FAMOUS ANONYMOUS

Morgan Baden

PIXEL+INK

PIXEL✛INK

Pixel+Ink is an imprint of TGM Development Corp.

Text copyright © 2025 by TGM Development Corp.
Jacket and title page illustration copyright © 2025 by Bex Glendining
All rights reserved. No part of this book may be reproduced, transmitted, or stored in an information retrieval system in any form or by any means, graphic, electronic, or mechanical, including photocopying, taping, and recording, without prior written permission from the publisher. Additionally, no part of this book may be used or reproduced in any manner for the purpose of training artificial intelligence technologies or systems, nor for text and data mining.
Printed and bound in July 2025 at Sheridan, Chelsea, MI, U.S.A.
Book design by Chelsea Hunter
www.pixelandinkbooks.com
First Edition

1 3 5 7 9 10 8 6 4 2

Library of Congress Cataloging-in-Publication Data is available.

ISBN: 978-1-64595-269-5 (hardcover)

EU Authorized Representative: HackettFlynn Ltd, 36 Cloch Choirneal, Balrothery, Co. Dublin, K32 C942, Ireland. EU@walkerpublishinggroup.com

For M and B and all the amazing kids on our block

HOUSE RULES

1. No leaving the house. Open the door ONLY for the pizza delivery!
2. Keep your hands to yourselves. (That means NO FIGHTING, Sophie and Gus!)
3. No DMing celebrities. (That one is for Harper!) In fact, no social media at all. Stay off your devices, maybe. Try to *talk* to each other.
4. No soccer practice in the house.
5. Video games are fine, but be reasonable about the hours you spend playing them, Luke.
6. To those who knock over any more lamps with your backflips: The cost *will* be taken out of your allowance!
7. Pizzas are set to be delivered at six. That means you do NOT need to Seamless or DoorDash or Uber Eats anything else. We *will* see the email receipt!
8. If you feel like eating something healthy, there's salad in the fridge!

BONUS RULE: Just . . . be safe, and be smart. We love you!

CHAPTER ONE
Sophie

The rules were simple.

We should have been able to follow them. No sweat, right? I mean, we weren't little kids anymore. We didn't even *need* rules!

But then . . .

Well, things got a teeny bit out of control. Just, like, a smidge. And we kind of ended up becoming famous.

A little.

And then . . . a lot.

And that's when things really went off the rails.

★★★

It all started on a regular Friday afternoon. The sun was bright, the sky was blue, my shorts were orange (my signature color), and an entire weekend stretched out before us. School was out, and we were on our way home!

"Over to you, Luke!" Gus Magee, my just-barely-younger brother, called.

Without waiting for Luke to respond, Gus kicked his ever-present soccer ball straight toward Luke Gage-Flashman.

But Luke, per usual, had his head buried in technology. He was somehow carrying a laptop while he walked, balancing it with his backpack and a water tumbler. I don't think he even heard Gus call his name.

Harper, Luke's just-barely-younger sister, was usually his spokesperson in social situations, since Luke was a kid of few words. But Harper was fresh out of drama class, and she was busy, well, being Harper.

"La, la, laaa!" she trilled, flinging out her arms and twirling around on the front lawn of Valleyville Junior High. Around us, kids streamed from the school's front doors and across the grass—just your typical after-school chaos.

"Look out!" I yelled. But it was too late. Gus's stupid soccer ball was headed straight for Luke. And while I wasn't the best math student in the world, I *had* gotten a solid B- in Geometry, so I knew a little something about angles. From what I could tell, the ball was going to ricochet off Luke's laptop and then bounce—*bam!*—right into Harper's face.

The very face that was tilted up toward the sky, hitting a high note. Oblivious.

Did I have to do *everything* around here?

The ball crashed into Luke's screen, but Luke held on. Then I dashed forward and took a flying leap, jumping as high as I could, landing between Luke and his sister. The ball crashed right into my ribs instead of Harper's open mouth.

"Ow," I moaned. That stung.

Harper flashed me a dazzling smile. "Nice moves, Soph!"

I shrugged. As the shortest person in seventh grade, I was pretty good at jumping higher than people expected. It was a survival mechanism. *You* try being twelve and looking like you're still a third grader.

Gus scooped up his ball while Luke closed his laptop to prevent further damage. He slipped it into his backpack and plopped big headphones over his ears.

Then the four of us continued silently down the hilly slope of the junior high and across the street.

The walk home from school took about ten minutes, and on a warm, fresh day like this, it was easy to see why all our parents were so proud to live in Valleyville. We were a quick train ride to the city, and lots of adults commuted there every day. But Valleyville itself felt like an old-fashioned village out of a television show: parks and cafés and hundred-year-old houses with leafy trees and old slate sidewalks where kids left drawings in chalk. On the other side of school was a small downtown area, with restaurants and shops and—obviously most important—the best smoothie place around.

Spring was springing, with bursts of flowers, and none of us were wearing our coats. Maybe we wouldn't need them till fall!

"Know what I just realized?" Harper said, breaking a silence with a gasp. "We haven't done this in *forever*!"

"Done what?" Luke mumbled. Apparently, he heard us through noise-canceling headphones?

"Walk home together!" Harper sang out; it was some kind of big reveal.

What was she even talking about? Harper and I walked home

together a couple times a week, depending on her acting classes. On the days she was busy, I walked with Gus.

But Harper meant all four of us, together.

"You mean the Rowan Roadies?" Gus said as we crossed over Main Street and turned left.

Harper beamed. "Rowan Roadies? Haven't heard that in a while!"

I took a deep breath, bracing myself for the uphill section of our walk home. The center of town was flat like a valley—Valleyville, remember?—but the farther out you ventured, the higher the ground rose. These hills were great for wintertime sledding, but not so fun when you had to walk home with a heavy backpack boring into your shoulders.

You're probably wondering, what on earth are Rowan Roadies? Well, *we* are. Or at least, we were.

See, Gus and I live right next door to Luke and Harper on a short street called Rowan Road. We're the same ages: Luke and me, both twelve and in seventh grade, and Gus and Harper, both eleven and in sixth. Our houses are almost identical. And our parents? They're not just neighbors, they're best friends.

When we were babies, people called the four of us "the adorable four." As toddlers, we were "the fearsome foursome." (Gus, in particular, was a terror.) And once we were old enough to roam the street by ourselves, on foot and on scooter, playing hide-and-seek and climbing over fences, someone started calling us the Rowan Roadies, and it stuck.

Harper and I were paired together a lot as kids, since we were both girls and people assumed we liked all the same things. But Luke was actually the one who became my best friend. On our first day of kindergarten, he was the one who convinced me to stop crying. When we were seven and I broke my ankle trying a triple back tuck on the driveway, he was the one who held my hand the whole drive to the hospital. And when we were seven and he was diagnosed with autism, I paid super-close attention to everything his moms said about how I could help him.

The four of us were *tight* and we looked out for each other fiercely. Sure, we had other friends at school, but at home it was like no other kids existed. The Rowan Roadies crashed in each other's bedrooms and never rang doorbells. Each set of sibs had a bonus set of parents. On hot summer days, we ran lemonade stands together, and on winter weekends, we built snowmen in each other's yards. Luke and Harper's moms stocked up on Gus's favorite protein bars, and our parents had an extra EpiPen on hand for Luke's peanut allergy. Some days, I even pretended Luke was my brother, instead of soccer-smelly Gus. One year, I truly thought it would make sense for Gus and Luke to switch bedrooms, so I spent a whole Sunday afternoon trying to push Gus's dresser down the second-floor hallway, where I planned—I half remember—to simply roll it down the stairs. When Mom caught me and explained why it wasn't going to happen, I cried. Hard.

We spent years like that, almost unaware that we weren't related. Until . . .

Well, it was hard to say exactly *what* happened.

Maybe it was that Gus had a knack for kicking balls and running superfast, so our dad signed him up for classes and coaches and soccer camps, until his afternoons and weekends were way too packed for the rest of us.

Or maybe it was that Harper's moms noticed her flair for the dramatic, and soon she was trying out for shows and taking multiple kinds of music lessons.

Then Luke needed after-school occupational therapy and other extra supports, and soon he was way more into taking apart old computers and playing video games than hanging out with boring old me.

I was still available, but suddenly I was all alone, and the Rowan Roadies were ancient history. We were still neighbors, but not exactly friends. And now it felt a little awkward.

I glanced up at Luke. Even though I was two months older than him, he was a full head taller than me now, his arms and legs all long and gangly. With his face still focused on his screen, it was hard to tell what he was thinking. Funny that I used to think I could read his mind.

Luke piped up, surprising us. "There's a reason we never walk home together," he announced. He pushed his glasses up the bridge of his nose and looked pointedly at Gus and Harper. "You two are never around!"

Harper's eyes bugged out. "Lukas Gage-Flashman! How dare you call me out like that! I can't help it if I have lessons after school! Hollywood waits for no one!"

"Drama queen," Luke said.

"He's not wrong," Gus pointed out. "I can't remember the last time I had a Friday afternoon without practice."

Yeah, they were all practicing something. Not me, though, because I hadn't quite decided what my "thing" was. I'd tried lots of activities, from tennis to swimming to pottery to coding to karate and gymnastics.

My problem wasn't in the trying; it was in the sticking.

But someday I'd find what I loved. Right?

I tried to push that nagging thought away. "Yeah, why don't you have practice today?" I asked my brother, elbowing him. "Did Coach realize how much you stink and kick you off the team?"

"If only," Gus sighed. Which didn't make any sense, because he loved soccer. Maybe that's why he dropped his ball to the ground just then, testing out some fancy footwork. The ball flew to the end of the block, landing right in front of the house on the corner.

Harper sang a creepy tune under her breath. "Dun-dun-dunnn!"

Luke laughed, but I could hear his hesitation. And despite the bright sunshine, I shivered.

Last year, the crumbling old structure that had been on the corner forever was torn down, and a new house—so modern it looked like it belonged in outer space—had appeared practically overnight. No one knew who lived in it, or even if anyone did.

The whole place was a mystery. And everyone knows what kids do when we don't have answers to something—we make up nicknames and scary stories. That's why every kid near Rowan Road called the place The Black Hole. Everything about it was just . . . empty.

I took a flying leap over the walkway to avoid touching the sidewalk in case it was cursed. Then we rounded the corner and turned up Rowan Road, where I could see the silhouette of two adults talking in our driveway.

Tara, one of Harper and Luke's moms, was chatting with my dad (James, if you were curious), and they both waved. It was weird to see my dad out there in the middle of a workday.

Most afternoons, he was on a call or presenting slides or whatever it was adults did all day in their home offices.

"What's up?" I asked, immediately suspicious.

My dad kissed my forehead and chuckled. "Hi to you, too. Hey, bud," he added, tousling Gus's dark brown hair.

Tara said, "So . . . remember how Ayana was supposed to watch you all tomorrow night?" For weeks, our parents had been excited about this fancy party Tara's law firm was throwing on Saturday night. My mom had even made my dad get a new suit. And Ayana, a college kid who'd been sitting for us for years, had agreed to watch us. It would be sort of like old times, but sort of not. I couldn't remember the last time we'd had a babysitter.

Ayana knew the funniest jokes and built the coolest playlists. Plus, she baked the most delicious brownies . . . from scratch, without a recipe! I wasn't jealous of her or anything.

"Unfortunately, she's come down with strep throat," my dad said, sighing.

"Bummer," Gus said. He shrugged off his backpack and it landed on the cement with a *thud*. He began kicking his soccer ball against the small retaining wall that kept the grass in our front lawn from spilling onto the sidewalk. "So who'd you get in her place?"

"Well, that's the problem," my dad said, crossing his arms and glancing nervously at Tara. "So far, everyone we've asked is busy, or traveling, or—"

"Or just doesn't want to spend their Saturday night watching four kids who are way too old to be babysat?" Harper said pointedly.

"Yeah!" I added, surprised that hadn't occurred to me before. "We don't need a sitter. Come on. I'm *twelve*."

But my dad and Tara tossed around a few potential babysitter names while I grew more and more worried, shifting my weight from foot to foot, like my shoes were too tight. I glanced at the others. Gus was kicking his ball around, as always, and Luke was still shutting out the world with his headphones. Only Harper seemed as frustrated as I was. When we locked eyes, she raised her eyebrows as if to say, *Do something!*

So I did.

"You know, the kids in the Baby-Sitters Club books were all my age. And they built an entire company!" I pointed out.

My dad looked charmed, at least. "That's cute, Soph."

"I'm not trying to be cute," I retorted.

"Sophie's right," Gus said. He kicked up his ball and caught it, spinning it in his fingers. "Why can't Luke and Harper come hang at our house? We'll just order pizza and chill."

"We won't even leave the living room!" Harper held up a hand like she was taking an oath.

"I'm sure there's someone else we can ask," Tara said. She began scrolling through her phone's contact list with a faint whiff of desperation.

Then the sound of a bike whizzing down our hilly street broke the silence.

"Yoda-lay-hee-hoo!" someone called out.

It was Olivia, a freshman at Valleyville High School who lived at the top of Rowan Road. She coasted down the hill, her dark hair flying behind her, and waved.

"Olivia!" Tara brightened. She nudged my dad's arm. "She'd be perfect!"

No way.

Olivia was only a little older than all of us, for one thing. But the main problem with her was that she was bossy. Not babysitter bossy, which is an acceptable kind (sometimes), but annoyingly bossy, like she thought she knew better than us about everything. Which she definitely did not!

"She does seem mature," my dad said, nodding.

Did he not remember how, last time she'd sat for us, she'd burned the microwave popcorn so badly that the smell lingered for days? Or that she'd laughed so hard at something Luke said that she'd snorted orange soda out of her nose?! The truth was, all the kids in the neighborhood felt the same way about her. She had a real reputation. And not the Taylor Swift kind!

Tara waved her over. "Do you have a sec?"

"Sure do!" Olivia sang-hollered. Then she lifted both hands from her handlebars, resting them on her hips. As someone who hadn't yet mastered the skill of riding my bike without holding the handles, I have to admit, I was impressed.

Until . . .

As Olivia got closer, her front wheel hit a small rock.

And because she wasn't holding on, she lost control of the bike.

And the bike curved left, straight toward us. *Screeeeeech!*

Olivia's bike hit the Gage-Flashmans' mailbox. Olivia tumbled over the handlebars and landed on the grass, crushing a purple hyacinth. Then she hopped to her feet like nothing had happened, while her bike wheels spun round and round.

"Honey, are you okay?!" Tara cried, rushing toward her. But Olivia just shrugged, giggling. She was fine. The hyacinth, not so much.

"All good! I'm always falling like that!" Olivia shrugged. "Woo! So klutzy!"

"Yeah," Tara said.

"Whoops." Olivia examined the palms of her hands, which were a little dirty and maybe a little bloody. She brushed them on her jeans and shrugged again. "I swear, I'm the least observant person on the planet! Like, I cannot be trusted to be alone!"

Harper snorted. Gus sighed. Luke's eyes grew very wide.

"So, what was it you wanted to ask me?" Olivia asked.

My dad stepped forward with a fake smile. "Never mind, Olivia. It can wait."

"Okay!" Olivia said. "Well, see you around!"

She hopped back on her bike, tucked her hair behind her ears, and disappeared down the hill.

The adults had one of those silent conversations using only their eyes.

Harper burst into a giggle. "Mom, I've never seen you speechless!"

"Should we try her again later or . . ." My dad's voice trailed off.

"Mom," Luke said, training his eyes on Tara. "Seriously, we can take care of ourselves. What's the worst that could happen?"

She let out a long sigh. She eyed each of us kids. Finally, she smiled. "Don't make us regret this," she said.

"Woo-hoo!" Harper's cheer echoed down Rowan Road.

I was so excited, I grabbed whoever was closest to me, squeezing their arm and squealing with delight. As soon as I realized it was Luke, though, I dropped his arm like a hot potato. We didn't have that kind of connection anymore.

As the parents talked details, we kids tried to play it cool. Still, the inside of my stomach felt funny. The four of us hadn't spent more than a couple minutes together—alone—in a long time. What would it feel like to be *forced*, basically, to hang out again?

Maybe I was worrying over nothing.

Maybe I was the only one acting sus, as kids from school liked to say.

Maybe it would all be okay, I thought. Like old times, even.

The wild thing was, I didn't hate it.

CHAPTER TWO
Gus

I'm a soccer star. I'm not bragging; it's a fact. I've been playing since I was three, and sometime around second grade, my coaches decided I had it. You know . . . *it*. That mysterious ingredient that turns casual players into professionals. Into stars.

And my life has been all soccer, all the time, ever since.

That Friday afternoon should've felt really special. I should've been celebrating!

It was the first Friday in forever that I had the afternoon completely free. Coach had canceled soccer practice because of flooding on the field. Then I'd finally won a (small) battle with my parents about being too old for a babysitter. Also, I knew Dad was making his world-famous chili for dinner.

But instead of being pumped, I stomped up the stairs and flung my backpack onto my desk. I tried to push all thoughts of soccer out of my brain, but in a bedroom like this, that was impossible.

I had something else on my mind.

I flopped onto my bed and pulled out the note that had been burning a hole in my back pocket all day, using one of my stupid soccer-ball pillows to prop up my head. Underneath me was my bedspread, in the black-and-white pattern of a ball; underneath my bed was my rug, the bright green of a field; surrounding me on my walls were posters of Pelé and Beckham and Hamm and Ronaldo and Rapinoe. Even the aquarium, where my pet turtle, Messi, lived, was decorated with little plastic soccer balls.

It was like soccer had thrown up all over my room.

Taking a deep breath, I opened the note that Mr. Hassan, my English teacher, had given to me that morning.

Congratulations! You've been selected as the sixth-grade Outstanding Creative Writing Student of the Year! This prestigious honor means you qualify for the Valleyville Writing Intensive, our summer camp for aspiring writers, and will have your work featured in a variety of channels online and in print. Please complete the attached form with your parent or guardian's signature and return it to your English teacher by May 1 to reserve your spot. We can't wait to see what you create this summer!

"Yo, bro!"

I dropped the note, buried it under my blanket, and bolted upright. "You have to knock, Sophie!"

But my sister was already halfway over the threshold. "Sorry," she said. "But, the good news is, Mom sent me to tell you to do your homework, and I pretended I didn't even hear her. You're welcome!"

I snorted. "Mom and her obsession with doing homework on Friday afternoons."

"Yeah, she's a hoot," Sophie agreed. "Then again . . . it does feel good to get it out of the way . . ."

"You know what else feels good?" I dramatically stretched my hands up and faked a long, loud yawn. Then I plopped my head back on my pillow and closed my eyes. "A late afternoon nap!"

"So true." Sophie nodded. She dived onto my bed, arranging herself until she was cross-legged next to me, her back resting against the wall.

I popped one eye open. "I'm sorry, did you think that was an invitation?"

She huffed, but she was smiling. She grabbed one of the soccer-ball pillows and threw it at me, but I easily caught it and tucked it behind my neck. *Such* an amateur.

Then, just as I had closed my eyes again to relish the feeling of freedom, I heard a crinkling.

Sophie had found my note. You know, the one I was trying to keep *secret*.

I jumped to my feet. "I can explain!"

But Sophie looked kind of . . . impressed. "You won a writing award? Bruh!" she said.

"Shhh!" I raced to the door, swiveling my head around to make sure no one was listening. Luckily, the coast was clear.

Sophie pushed her hair out of her eyes. "This is so cool!"

"Quiet," I urged. "Pretend you never saw this!"

Sophie, frowning, tossed the note back to me. "I don't get it. This is a big deal!"

I scrunched it up and shoved it into the top drawer of my desk. "Nah," I said. "It's not."

But that was the thing about sisters. Sometimes they knew just what to say—and by *that*, I mean what *not* to say. Because it *was* a big deal, and I wasn't sure what to do. I was Gus Magee, soccer star. Not Gus Magee, writer. Didn't Sophie know what our parents would say if I told them about this? It would go something like:

You can't go to the summer writing program, Gus. That's the same week as tryouts for the summer travel soccer team. And you can't miss the summer travel soccer team, because that's what makes you eligible for the fall travel soccer team. And that *is the team that feeds into the varsity program at the high school, which you need to make so that recruiters start noticing you by sophomore year, so that . . .*

My whole life was already planned out. And it revolved entirely around a little black-and-white ball.

Soccer made me, me. And yet . . . the more I loved it, the less time and space I had for other parts of me.

I shifted uncomfortably under Sophie's gaze. One thing about my sister: She has these really big, shiny eyes. Like, cartoon-character eyes. She was staring. And let me tell you, if you ever had Sophie stare at *you*, you'd understand the pressure I felt to tell her the truth.

Finally, she broke her gaze. "Gus, why are you acting weird about this? Isn't this a good thing?"

I shrugged and kicked the corner of the stupid green rug where it curled up at the end. I'd tripped on that corner about a million times.

"You know me, Soph," I finally said. "Every minute I spend writing is a minute I don't spend on soccer."

"Why can't you do both? Mom and Dad let me try all sorts of things!"

I shook my head. Our parents were different with me, probably because soccer had been my "thing" since forever. It was too late to change my thing! "You don't get it, Soph. Trust me. This is bad."

After a long sigh, Sophie gave up her line of questioning. "Okay. If you say so," she said. "Anyway! What should we do tomorrow night?"

We?

"Luke and I will probably play a video game," I began.

Sophie frowned. "That means I'll be stuck with Harper? Come on! You know she's gonna force me to read lines or act out some kind of skit with her or something!"

I shrugged again.

A glint began to shine in Sophie's eyes. They were less cartoony now, more like let's-make-a-deal.

"How about I'll keep your secret if you and Luke keep Harper off my back tomorrow night?" Sophie said.

My jaw dropped. "That's blackmail!"

She stuck out her hand. "Potato, po-tah-to. Deal?"

At the mention of potatoes, my stomach growled.

The sooner I got Sophie out of here, the sooner I could go raid the kitchen, and the sooner she'd forget we ever talked about this.

I thought about the options in front of me. If Sophie told our parents, all I'd hear about was how summer soccer was so "critical to my future." Mom loved to talk about how I "dedicated myself fully to the sport." Half of her phone calls to Grandma and Grandpa were bragging about my recent wins. And she never let the rest of us forget that they were counting on soccer scholarships to help fund my college education.

As for my dad . . . after coming to every soccer match of my lifetime, he'd recently decided to join my team as a volunteer assistant coach. It shouldn't have been a surprise—after all, he was the guy who came to every home game waving a Valleyville pennant in the air and wearing a T-shirt with my picture on it. (Exactly as embarrassing as it sounds!) But it meant that now, especially, was not the time to raise the idea of distractions from the game.

Yeah, most parents would probably be thrilled if their kid had won a writing award. Like, if Luke or Harper had won? Tara and Brynn would throw them a party! But my parents had already put so much into soccer, and only soccer, that I was afraid this might break their brains. Or worse, their hearts.

What choice did I have? Sighing, I shook Sophie's hand.

CHAPTER THREE
Harper

I knew there would be rules, but a laminated poster that listed them was a bit MUCH. Still, that's exactly what someone had slipped under my bedroom door overnight. I read it and gasped. No direct-messaging celebrities on the one social media app my moms let me use? Did they want me to PERISH FROM BOREDOM?

I knew exactly who had made this list: Mom B. Who was, somewhat ironically, given her name, *very* Type A. She'd even added everyone's phone numbers at the bottom of the list (did she think we didn't know our OWN PARENTS' phone numbers?), the address and number of the restaurant they would all be at for the night (has she heard of Google?!), and—I'm not kidding—the words *In an emergency, call 9-1-1* highlighted in red.

No wonder I was so dramatic. It was CLEARLY GENETIC!

I snapped a pic of the printout and texted it to Luke, Sophie, and Gus with a cry-laugh emoji. Sophie responded with the poop emoji, which was very on brand.

Mom B's intensity was no secret. It wasn't that she didn't trust us, exactly—more that she dealt with crises all day as part of her job in politics, so she couldn't help imagining the ways things might go wrong *outside* of work, too. Even in Valleyville.

Speaking of Valleyville, you could catch a train here and be in the city in half an hour. So close, and yet so far! Within thirty minutes, you could be surrounded by skyscrapers and musicals and enough people to make your head spin. My first memories of the city are of looking up at a theater marquee and thinking, "I want MY name up there one day!"

But I'm getting off track here.

In order to catch the train that would get them to the party on time, my moms and the Magees needed to leave Rowan Road by 4:45 sharp. That meant that, by four-thirty that Saturday, Mom T was ringing the Magees' doorbell while the rest of us crowded behind her on the front stoop.

My moms looked fancy. Mom T was in a navy cocktail dress, and Mom B was in a cool floral jumpsuit that I made a mental note to borrow once I was tall enough. Luke was carrying his Switch and his headphones. Me? I just had my backpack stuffed with a few necessities: some face masks I was hoping Sophie would do with me, the script for the *Beauty and the Beast Jr.* musical so I could practice for next week's big auditions (BELLE OR BUST!). Plus a few other odds and ends to get us through the night.

Sophie and Gus's mom, Kira, opened the door. "Come in, come in!" she said. I flashed my most confident smile. While I had practically lived here as a little kid, it had been ages since I'd been inside. (Maybe they had finally painted the walls ELECTRIC PINK, like I had long ago suggested!)

She gestured us inside, and Luke and I practically fell over each other to be the first one in. I peered around him and then our moms to survey the Magees' house. Sadly, no electric pink paint could be seen, which was a real MISSED OPPORTUNITY, if you asked me. But it was nice, too, that the house looked just as I remembered: cozy and cramped, with a pile of sports equipment on the floor, a messy blanket on the couch, a big half-eaten bowl of popcorn on the coffee table. In fact, the familiarity practically brought a TEAR to my eye!

As Sophie and Gus wandered into the living room from the kitchen, I noticed Kira's outfit. I whistled. "Okay, Beyoncé! Slay!"

She grinned and bowed in response. Like my moms, Kira was dressed up. Her long, dark braids were gathered on the crown of her head, and she wore a pair of heels so high that she towered over us all. I'd dressed for the occasion, too, wearing my favorite dress (yellow and green stripes) with pink polka-dot leggings and my shiny gold cowboy boots. What can I say? My fans appreciated a LEWK. Unlike Mom B, Kira always complimented me on my fashion experiments, and I could tell she REALLY meant it.

Just then, James bounded down the stairs in a navy-blue suit.

"Ooh, James Bond!" I teased him. "You headed to the Academy Awards, big shot?"

"Dial it back, Harper," Luke muttered. But I couldn't help it! Giving compliments was a surefire way of putting people at EASE. And by the looks on Sophie's and Gus's faces, I could tell not everyone was feeling ease-y about the night ahead. Maybe we were all a little anxious about how we would gel.

There was an awkward silence among us kids, but our parents were gabbing nonstop. Then I felt something fuzzy brush past my leg. I glanced down and gasped. "Poodle!"

"Harper!" Mom T sighed.

"Not again," said Mom B.

My cat, Poodle, who was the MOST adorable cat you've ever seen, with black and gray markings and bright green eyes and a real knack for appearing in places she shouldn't be, must have followed us out our front door and across the driveway to the Magees'. And then—WHOOPS!—inside their front door, which I might have accidentally left open. Quick as a flash, Poodle snuck between my legs and darted up their staircase!

Now, as long as I'd known Kira, she'd never been a cat person. But she'd always been a *cool* person. So she shrugged and said, "I learned long ago that Poodle is a package deal with you, kiddo," which made me feel even prouder to be Poodle's mama.

"I promise I won't let her destroy anything," I said, grinning.

James clapped his hands together. "Well, we've got to catch the train. Kids, any questions?"

Gus shook his head. I shrugged. Luke looked bored.

Sophie jumped in. "Nope! I think we're good! The list of rules was really helpful, Brynn!"

Mom B looked pleased. But I crinkled my eyebrows, which was a new thing I was trying after realizing my face wasn't as EXPRESSIVE as an actor's should be. Sophie noticed, and I mouthed to her, *"What?"* She just shrugged.

Which reminded me.

"Oh, hey, look!" I pulled my microphone from my backpack and wiggled my eyebrows again. "Who likes karaoke?"

"Annnnnd, that's our cue," Mom T said.

It took four full minutes for them to leave. "Call us anytime! I mean it! Literally, for anything!" Mom B pleaded. Mom T kissed our foreheads a million times. Last-minute, James realized his shoes were too tight and had to go change them, and then Kira had to apply her lipstick again. It was a whole THING.

Finally, the door closed behind them.

"Well, that was annoying," Gus muttered. "It's just a few hours."

"Overkill," Sophie agreed.

"Parents." Luke shook his head.

As for me? I beamed.

We were free.

★★★

The pizza came right on time, just as we were in the middle of the latest Marvel movie. I was multitasking and reading the *Beauty and the Beast Jr.* script between fight scenes, but I took a break from memorizing Belle's lines to inhale a couple slices. They tasted like a memory; of all the things I'd eaten in the Magees' house, I'd probably eaten pizza the most.

Then Sophie ripped open a bag of chips, and Gus passed out more soda, and I suddenly remembered how Kira had a massive sweet tooth and liked to hide her treats at the bottom of the freezer, underneath the peas. Everyone cheered when I uncovered the box of ice cream sandwiches, which we quickly demolished.

Things were totally normal. And by normal I mean we were FINE without parents, because of course we were. And also, like, we were back to the way things always used to be. The four of us, just hanging in someone's house, goofing off.

Why had we stopped, again?

Anyway, as soon as the credits rolled, and I mean the REAL end of the credits, after the post-credits scene, we were all ready for something new to do.

My brother nodded at Gus. "I brought *After Launch*."

"Sa-weet!" Gus jumped up from the couch and rubbed his hands together.

Luke had been saving up for *After Launch* for months. It was some new and hugely popular online game that kids at school couldn't stop talking about, and I'd seen it being played all over my social media. I PERSONALLY didn't understand why people chose to watch animated characters when they could spend their time studying real people AUTHENTICALLY EMOTE on screen instead, but I'd always been told I was the odd one out here.

They started heading upstairs when Sophie began clearing her throat and coughing.

"Omigod! Are you choking on a Twizzler?" I said. Even Poodle, who'd reappeared after taking a tour of the house, looked concerned.

But Sophie kept going, her cough growing louder—and, weirdly, in only Gus's direction.

"Soph!" I yelled. Poodle jumped, along with Sophie. "I know CPR! Luke, call 9-1-1!"

She immediately stopped. Her cheeks were pink. "No, no, I'm good. It's just . . ."

"You practically DIED!" I wailed.

Sophie glared at Gus. And then, like he suddenly understood something the rest of us didn't, he nodded and slumped back down the stairs.

Luke turned around. "Gus?" he called. "You coming?"

"I . . . uh . . . what if Sophie plays with us?" he said.

What?!

"No can do!" I chirped. I held up my phone and beamed at Sophie. I knew she didn't want to play some dumb video game with our brothers! I would SAVE her. "I have that big audition this week," I explained. "And I need Sophie's help running through some lines!"

Sophie's eyes flashed. Maybe someone else would've said Sophie looked STRICKEN, but I thought she looked INTRIGUED.

"But, Harper, I really want to see *After Launch*," Sophie pleaded. "It's such a cool game and I've been wanting to play it, like, forever!"

I frowned. She was being way too NICE to Luke. Another thing that was just like old times. But girls needed to stick together! "Excuse me, but since when do you play video games?"

Suddenly, she kicked Gus. He winced but hurried to answer for her. "Uh, she's been playing with me. At home. Sometimes."

Luke looked mildly interested. "Really?" he said.

Something wasn't adding up. "Oh yeah? So, what's the game about?"

Gus started to speak, but I shushed him. "*Sophie*," I said pointedly. "What's it about?"

Her eyes darted back and forth to the boys. "Um. It's . . . an online game . . . where you have to . . . like, win . . . and stuff."

Gus groaned, but Luke stepped in to help. "She's kind of right," he said. And then, in my brother's typical way, he explained the whole thing, sounding like he'd memorized the description from the game's marketing team.

"*After Launch* is the hottest online game in the world right now! It's a cooperative strategy and combat game in which players take on the role of human explorers who, after launching from their Earth base, discover that an alien race called the Lorgans have established a massive blockade of Earth!"

Lorgans. Aliens. WHO CARED?

Luke went on. "The explorers can't go home, but there's no help coming, either. So the players must take the fight directly to the Lorgans and eventually find and destroy their home base, which is hidden in the black hole at the center of the Milky Way!"

I blinked. "Oh."

But Luke still wasn't done. He held up two fingers and checked them off one by one. "Combat is multiphased," he said, his voice shaking a little the way it did whenever he was excited about something. "Players collaborate to operate their space vessel, retrofitting it from a science ship into a warship. They engage with Lorgan ships— first one at a time, but eventually with multiple ships at once—in vessel-to-vessel combat! And once a Lorgan ship is disabled, players can choose to destroy it, or put on their vac-suits and spacewalk to the ship, engaging in combat with the crew. If victorious, they can plunder the ship for alien technology to upgrade their own vessel!"

As Luke caught his breath, we all stared at him in silence. Finally, Gus cleared his throat. "Yeah. What he said."

I threw my hands up in the air. "What, so you're all going to ABANDON me while you try to fight some aliens?"

Then I sighed as deeply as I could, letting all the breath out of me like my theater coach made me do before auditions. A good scene partner knows when to surrender to the other characters. "Fine. I'll play, too."

Luke laughed until I shot him a look. "Oh. You're . . . serious?" he said.

"Don't you hate video games?" Gus asked.

"I have many talents! Maybe gaming is one of my undiscovered ones!" I said loftily.

Sophie and Gus looked troubled, but that was probably because they were SCARED of my potential prowess at kicking their alien butts. That's the effect a little confidence can have.

"Fine," Luke grumbled. "Let's use the big TV in here, then, instead of my computer."

I followed Luke's lead as he set up the game, which by the way was DIFFICULT for a born leader like me, and soon all four of us were sprawled on the couch and floor, holding controllers and listening as Luke explained what to do. I looked around and realized the four of us had probably sat in these exact same positions a thousand times.

Now, was the storyline of the game interesting? Not quite. As an actor, I'd never quite fallen in love with the science fiction genre. But it got me thinking about how we ALL feel like aliens sometimes, and how I could USE this material to better tap into my emotions in my upcoming audition!

You see, EVERYTHING can be an acting lesson.

Luke pressed some more buttons, and we each started choosing our characters. "I've only played twice, so I haven't gotten very far," Luke said as we all clicked away. "So we can start over as a team. It's more fun that way anyhow."

As a team . . . just like we were in the old days. I nearly TEARED UP! As an actor, my emotions were always close to escaping, but this was a bit much, even for me. I cleared my throat and tried to focus.

"I've heard the final battle is sick!" Gus said.

"Battle?" I repeated. They all knew I wasn't a huge fan of violence.

Sophie patted my arm. "It's just alien stuff. It doesn't look real or anything."

I shot her a grateful look.

"So far, no one's announced that they've defeated the Lorgans," Luke said.

"If anyone can, it's us," Gus declared.

I grinned. Gus had always been a team player. That's part of what made him so great at soccer!

Luke clicked around a bit more, explaining the basics. The longer he spoke, the more he seemed to come alive. He really liked this game!

Then he held up his hands as if to say *Ta-da*, which by the way was one of my signature moves, and we all started to play.

I tried to get into it. I really did. But it was a LOT of intergalactic stuff that all kind of blended together. Outer space was so dark. Where were the rainbows? The glitter? The light sources that served to highlight someone's flawless makeup?

There was one cool thing about the game, I guess: The aliens themselves were cute and charming, instead of scary. They danced and spun and giggled, even as they were attacking the astronauts. They had the most defined eyelashes I'd ever seen!

"Okay, this game is so SLAY! I love their costumes!" I marveled when a fresh wave of Lorgans flooded the screen, wiggling their creepy alien arms.

"They're not *costumes*," Luke corrected. "That's just the Lorgans' bodies!"

Suddenly, I had an idea. I snapped my fingers. As a result, okay, I dropped my controller, and my character died. Whoops! The others groaned, but my mind was already ten steps ahead of them.

"Be right back!" I called when I was halfway out the door.

I guess that means that TECHNICALLY I was the first person to break one of the rules.

And I guess that means—again, if we're speaking TECHNICALLY—that what happened next might have been my fault.

But can you blame me? If you saw how cute those *After Launch* aliens were, and how precisely they matched one of my costumes from a play I did a few years ago, you'd understand. It was fate! Kismet! Destiny!

It was also TROUBLE. Because if I hadn't gone back to my house to dig through my closet and find that costume, I wouldn't have had the idea to turn *After Launch* into a live-action video.

And none of the rest of this would have happened.

★★★

Luke, Sophie, and Gus were so focused on the game that they didn't hear me sneak back inside and creep up behind them. Their backs were to me, and I moved like a ninja, pulling the tripod from my backpack and positioning it so I had a perfect view of the entire living room. I paused to study them for a second, grinning to myself. It had been a while since Luke had gamed with people IRL. It was nice to see him in his element, and I was happy Gus and Sophie were witnessing it, too.

Man, was I HOT, though! I was in a shimmery silver unitard, skintight and thick. I pulled the hood up over my head so it covered my hair, made sure the silver lipstick I'd smeared all over my face was still there, and hit RECORD.

I looked JUST LIKE one of the cute little alien Lorgans!

While the others were hyper-focused, I crept behind them like a scene in a horror movie. As my phone recorded, with my friends none the wiser, I shimmied and slithered all around the living room, dancing and waving my arms for the camera and trying not to laugh. They had no idea I was behind them! And I really IMMERSED

MYSELF in the feeling of being an alien, stuck on a warship far from home with these messed-up, confusing humans!

If you ask me, it was a STAR performance.

"Ooh, good one," Gus suddenly exclaimed in response to something Luke had done in the game, and I jumped, thinking he'd caught me. But nope! They were deep in intergalactic battle, and they didn't know I was RIGHT THERE!

I pointed at them and silently laughed, looking directly at the camera so the audience (someday in the future) could get in on the joke.

And that got me thinking about a way to level up this video. After all, I am not famous for being SUBTLE.

With the phone still recording, I dropped to my hands and knees and slowly crawled on the floor to one side of the couch. I held my breath as I approached the side, my head peeking around the corner. I saw Sophie's bright red socks, so close I could have reached out and touched them. Luke was on the far end of the sofa, while Gus sat cross-legged on the floor between them.

Inside my head, I counted to three, and then I leaped to my feet. "BOO!"

"Aaaahhhhh!" Sophie's high-pitched scream rang out.

"Eeeuuuggghhh!" Luke yelled, throwing his controller into the air.

"STOP!" Gus demanded, jumping up in front of Sophie, as if to protect her.

I collapsed into a heap of giggles on the carpet.

And after a few seconds of stunned silence, they all did, too.

I've known since I was little that I was going to be famous. I've always just felt it in my bones. Acting, singing, dancing—they're what make me, ME. And that ME was going to be a performer someday.

But that night? I realized I'd been missing a key ingredient in my plans for future success.

ALL the best actors eventually become directors, right? What had I been thinking—or rather, NOT THINKING—by not honing my directing skills at the same time?!

Luke and Gus tried to act like they hadn't been scared by my alien cosplay, but I had it on video. "Gather round!" I called, resting my phone on the kitchen counter as everyone crowded behind me. Poodle joined us, too, and Gus absentmindedly scooped her up to cuddle. *Aw.* For a kid who'd been scared of animals, he'd come a long way.

I tapped PLAY.

Within seconds, Sophie got the giggles. And then Luke laughed, which, for my always-serious brother, was a real GIFT and a nod to my talents. If I do say so myself.

We kept watching, and even from my little phone screen, it was clear this video was GOLD. Imagine how it would look with some special effects!

Once the video ended, we watched it again. And then again after that.

"We left no crumbs!" Sophie marveled on the fourth viewing. "Who knew Lorgans could be so funny if you just made them dance a little more?" There in the kitchen, she started mimicking my alien moves, and my jaw dropped. Sophie looked pretty good! She matched my style really well. Almost like I had TRAINED her.

The three of us cheered as she kept going, and then Gus started dancing, too, only he must've known he didn't have the ACTUAL skills, so he was mostly imitating us. But *that* was hilarious, too!

Y'all . . . we were FUNNY. And our video? It was both creative and EPIC.

Luke didn't dance, but he did laugh, a lot. So much that he collapsed onto one of the kitchen stools, breathless.

I hadn't seen my brother this giddy in a long time. He was pretty used to masking at school, but at home, with just us, he could let loose and be himself. My heart was so full, I could feel it in my throat. I LOVED when the world got to see Luke the way I did!

And with that, another idea hit me.

"Here's the deal," I said. "We're putting on a show."

★★★

The next hour was a real whirlwind.

We decided to make an *After Launch*–themed mini-movie, where Sophie and I would dress as Lorgans and Gus and Luke would be the humans trying to steal a Lorgan ship. Spending the night like this was my DREAM COME TRUE . . . even if it wasn't exactly in line with the rules. Twice, I caught a glimpse of Mom B's laminated printout, sticking out of my backpack, as if it was taunting me.

But I carried on, fully committed to my ARTISTIC VISION.

It took some time to find costumes that could work. Sophie and Gus's older cousins gave them bags and bags of hand-me-downs over the years, and now they were stuffed into Sophie's closet. We found a treasure trove of barely used Halloween costumes and dance recital outfits! I sat cross-legged in the middle of Sophie's bedroom, surrounded by options. (With Poodle, who wanted to be a part of the action.) Under my direction, we made a quick mess of things, showering the floor with clothes as we sifted through the bags. I was so excited, I was practically vibrating.

"Those." I said, pointing at a pair of black platform boots.

"These?" Sophie looked troubled. "For the video?"

"Nope. For school. They are KILLER. They'll go with every outfit you own. The eighth-grade girls will think you're a fashion maven AND you'll be so confident. Wear them on Monday!"

Sophie frowned. "Hmm." But I noticed she didn't return them to the bag of costumes.

Next, she plucked a silver bodysuit out of the pile and held it up, her eyes hopeful.

"A thousand percent," I confirmed. "Perfect. Genius."

"Now for the pants . . ." Sophie rummaged through the mountain of costumes. After a moment, she yelled, "Jackpot!"

In her hands was a pair of sparkly gray leggings. Not quite a perfect match, and they were probably way too long, but we could make do.

"Go put them on while I figure out the boys," I ordered, surveying the scene. "There's gotta be something in here . . ."

As Sophie dashed to the bathroom to change, my brother groaned. He and Gus had been studying *After Launch* images on their phones near Sophie's bed, trying to find an easy hack for their homemade costumes. "Can't we just wear white hoodies or something?"

"I mean, you *could*," I pointed out. "If you wanted to look like amateurs."

In a shocking move, even Gus agreed with me. "Yeah, Luke. Did you see that sparkly thing Sophie's putting on? We can't let her show us up! Let's do this!"

Gus pocketed his phone and pulled out the final bag from the back of Sophie's closet. As he dumped it on the floor, something caught my eye.

"Wait a HOT MINUTE!" I suddenly yelled. I pointed.

Gus looked bewildered. "These just look like old superhero costumes."

"That's not a superhero!" I crawled over to his pile and triumphantly plucked up a long off-white jumpsuit with a recognizable patch on the arm. "That's a Ghostbuster!"

"No, that's *two* Ghostbusters," Luke announced, presenting an identical costume from the same bag.

"And if we remove these patches . . ." Gus continued, pulling at the threads of a patch. Luke's eyes lit up.

"They look pretty close to the vac-suits the humans wear in the game!" Luke realized.

Gus and Luke had always been able to finish each other's sentences as kids. Apparently, nothing had changed.

They both stepped into their suits. As I paced around the boys, figuring out where to pin and tuck and pull so the costumes would fit right, the door was flung open.

"Oh my gosh," Sophie squealed. "Look!"

She rocked her Lorgan outfit, and, to my utter SHOCK AND DELIGHT she wore a sleek black eye mask, dotted with silver sequins that feathered out over her cheekbones and forehead. Plus, she was triumphantly waving a matching one in her hand FOR ME.

I almost couldn't breathe, this was so perfect.

"We can't fight Lorgans without some head protection," Luke reminded Gus.

"And, like, oxygen masks," Gus added.

So, as Sophie smeared my silver lipstick on the parts of our faces the masks didn't cover, I helped the boys with the final stretch of our hunt. We somehow managed to construct helmet-type contraptions from old baseball caps and beanies, combined with posterboard and duct tape (in a last gasp of DESPERATION).

When we were all fully adorned, or as fully adorned as we could be without access to a proper costume department, we grouped together in front of the mirror on Sophie's closet door. And there, standing before us, were two OTHERWORLDLY alien creatures and two human-shaped things that could TOTALLY pass for astronauts. If you squinted.

In other words, we would do.

I directed us toward the Magees' attached garage, which, if memory served, had a neutral gray wall that I could totally turn into outer space in postproduction. (Luke agreed to help me figure out the specifics.) Luke fetched some of the special video equipment he kept in his room, while Sophie and Gus worked on lighting. Then, together, we mapped out a loose script. Just some general directions and ideas and stuff, so that all this costume work wouldn't be for nothing.

And when I yelled "Action!" I knew one thing.

THIS is what I was born to do: Put on a show.

Entertain people.

SHINE.

★★★

When it was over, we all collapsed on the random old couch in the garage, breathless. Even Poodle was exhausted! My hairline was all sweaty from my silver hood. I needed lemonade and Starburst, in that order.

But I was *proud*.

The two-minute video we'd created was epic. I could *feel* it. In the garage, we'd acted out the opening scene of *After Launch*, which was a quick, easy battle. But we hammed it up to be funny instead of serious. Then, Luke edited in the funniest clips from the earlier video I'd made, of my solo dancing and the big scare on the couch. Somehow, the final video just WORKED.

My acting coach always said we'd know when we nailed a scene. And she was right. Our video was a SMASH HIT. Or, at least, it would be, if anyone ever saw it.

Something clicked inside my brain. Like I could actually feel the gears turning.

Gus piped up. "Harper? I gotta be honest, I never understood why you cared so much about theater before."

"And now?" I arched an eyebrow.

"Now, I get it," he said simply.

Did I TEAR UP a little? Why, yes. Yes, I did.

"The moms would be really proud of me for being in front of the camera," Luke mused. And he was right. They didn't want him to fade into the background all the time.

"Too bad they're not gonna see it," Gus pointed out. "This video shows us breaking at least three different rules."

(Remember those rules from the beginning of this book? You know, the ones that VERY CLEARLY told us what we WERE and WERE NOT allowed to do?)

Sophie looked at the floor, where a camping lantern lay in pieces. She'd done a cartwheel the first time I'd yelled "Action!" and landed right on top of it!

"Yeah, that one was my bad," she said. "Our parents definitely cannot see this."

"But we can still watch the video ourselves," Luke suggested. "And then just . . . put it away in a folder on my laptop."

"Neat," Sophie said, brushing her curly dark hair off her forehead. "Cool."

Something about the WAY she said it made me wonder if she was for real.

I just nodded like I agreed with everything they were saying.

"Anyway, let's watch," Gus nodded, jiggling his foot like he was playing soccer without a ball.

"Show us what we did, Harp!" Luke threw a pillow at me. (Another rule broken!)

"You can't watch a movie without snacks," Sophie pointed out.

Five minutes later, we were all inside, water consumed, Dorito bag reopened, Poodle curled up on the couch. Then Gus turned on his laptop.

"In five, four, three, two . . ." he said, and hit PLAY.

★★★

The parents texted us all at a quarter to midnight, just as their train was pulling in to the Valleyville station. Sophie was asleep on the recliner in the corner of the living room, Luke was on his Switch, and Gus had disappeared up to his room an hour earlier. Poodle was still here, napping on my feet.

As for me, I'd been watching—and rewatching—our video on Gus's laptop, which he'd left on the dining room table.

I just couldn't push away the feeling that this thing was special.

That we—the four of us—made magic when we were together.

That the Rowan Roadies were quite possibly DESTINED to do this.

I wasn't thinking about the rules. Or about what it meant to post yourself online and open the floodgates.

So, with T-minus-eight minutes until our parents arrived home, I found my fingers tapping keys that led me directly to the most bussin' social media platform around: Cre8.

Cre8 was the place for short videos, usually set to music or a voiceover narration, that was super addictive and fun to watch. In fact, it was probably my favorite app of ALL TIME.

No one knew I had a Cre8 account. Because TECHNICALLY, I wasn't allowed.

BUT. I had a very good reason for this secret account.

See, a few months earlier, Selvi Gill, my biggest competition in the Valleyville Junior High theater department, claimed she'd been able to improve her acting skills by posting herself reciting famous monologues on Cre8 and incorporating feedback from viewers. And maybe I was a little JEALOUS that *I* hadn't thought of that. And a little worried that her acting skills would overtake mine. And then what? Surely, my moms wouldn't want me to lose a starring role to Selvi and relinquish all my dreams. They were VERY supportive of my art!

But they were NOT supportive of social media. In fact, they were pretty clear about it: no unsupervised social media accounts. Which is why my content on the other apps was SO boring, no matter how colorful I tried to make it. They had to approve every single post I made!

I hadn't posted anything on my Cre8 account yet. I just used it to lurk, mostly near Selvi. By following her acting journey, I'd figure out a way to stand out at our upcoming auditions!

But . . . everyone starts somewhere.

So, still buzzing from our video shoot, I logged into Cre8 with my untraceable password: PaDoodleCaboodle11.

As my fingers hovered over the UPLOAD button, I made a quick pro/con list in my head:

Pros:

We were completely anonymous! No one would know it was us.

The video was totally unique, and maybe it would make someone laugh.

Maybe it would make me famous! Er, I mean US. Make US famous.

This could be my BIG BREAK. And then I would DEFINITELY earn the part of Belle in the spring musical. And from there? FAME and FORTUNE!

Cons:

*I'm *technically* not supposed to have this social media account . . . but my moms would understand, once I signed my first film contract.*

We broke a few rules to film this video . . . but do our parents really sweat the details? They're busy people!

Then again, if they DO find out . . .

I didn't finish that last thought. No need to waste my CREATIVE VISION on the what-ifs.

On my tongue, I tasted buttered popcorn; a sure sign that I had to trust my INTUITION.

I heard the front door lock click open and the knob turn.

There was no time to waste. I tapped the button, I slammed the laptop closed, and I ran to the greet our parents, a thread of exhilaration growing through me like a long piece of shiny red licorice.

CHaPTeR FOUR
Luke

For some reason, there was a spotlight shining directly on me.

"Turn it off," I groaned, but my tongue felt too big, and the words didn't sound right. The light grew brighter.

I put all my effort into moving my arms, but I was stuck. I was swimming in glue and my limbs were frozen.

With a force, I jolted awake. I was just in bed. In my room. Status check: Everything was fine. I'd been dreaming. No—*nightmaring*. That's what Mom B used to call it, when I'd wake up in the middle of the night, crying and running to my moms' room.

I scratched my chin and rubbed my eyes. Usually, after a nightmare, my heart would be racing or I might even be sweating a little bit. But this time, my body was normal.

What if I wasn't actually nightmaring at all? I wondered. What if I was dreaming about being onstage, in the spotlight? Last night's *After Launch* movie had been pretty fun, I had to admit. I didn't normally like attracting attention. I wasn't my *sister*. But for that one shining moment . . . it wasn't so bad being watched by a camera. Or being part of a team again, in a way.

I stretched my arms up and yawned obnoxiously loud. *Was it obnoxiously loud?* I didn't know. That's just what Harper always said to me whenever I made a noise. I think it was her attempt at irony, since she was always so much louder than me.

Then I sat up in bed, wide awake. It was Sunday!

One weekend a month, Mom T and I challenged each other to a *Fortnite* match. Apparently, she'd been a total gamer when she was a kid (I know . . . I'm also shocked there were video games back then), and now it was kind of our thing.

Today was one of those Sundays. We'd eat a big, carb-filled breakfast and disappear into the basement for the entire morning, while Mom B and Harper did some kind of art project or gardening thing together.

I checked the clock—it was just after eight. Early! But I didn't want Mom T to forget about our plans, so I decided to text her in case she left to go grocery shopping or something else parents did on weekends.

What, like I was going to get out of bed and go downstairs? Nope. Not happening.

But when I picked up my phone, it was . . . on fire.

Not technically on fire. But it was hot. Because for some reason I had millions of notifications lighting up my home screen.

Okay, I don't have a ton of friends who text me. I mean, I have some friends—like, kids at school. And definitely on Twitch. But not *friends* friends, like Harper has.

It's just that I like doing things on my own, I guess. It's simpler for everyone involved. If I don't let people get too close to me, I don't have to explain all my rules (which are very, very different from Mom B's rules from last night). They make perfect sense in my head, to me! But I understand now that they don't always make sense to anyone else.

Let me back up a sec.

When I was younger, I was what my moms like to call *a handful*. I had specific processes I felt I had to follow all the time, even if they didn't seem obvious to anyone else. Certain clothes didn't feel right on my skin. Certain foods didn't feel right on my tongue. Sneakers with laces? Forget it. And even though she's younger than me, Harper actually began talking way before I did. (Literally *no one* is surprised if I tell them that now.) Eventually, my moms and my pediatrician stopped viewing all my quirks as just my personality and realized they added up to a different story. *My* story. The story of Luke Gage-Flashman, who is neurodivergent. (And a whole lot of other things, of course. But sometimes the neurodivergence feels like it needs to be the first thing I tell people.)

I'm still figuring out how much I need to explain, and when, and even *why*. But you don't really know me unless you know this thing about me.

Being diagnosed as neurodivergent meant that I got access to lots of supports in school, including a social skills class that I still think about now, even though I'm mostly okay about socializing these days if I have to. (I mean, I'm not like Harper, who can make friends with the yellowjacket that wants to sting her, but is *any*one like Harper?!) I learned some tools for staying physically regulated, which keeps me emotionally regulated.

What this all means is that I don't really want or need people the same way as other kids. I have my gaming buddies, I have Harper when I need her, and I have a couple kids at school who are into technology the way I am. And that's enough.

Or . . . it felt like enough, until last night, maybe. When the Rowan Roadies were back together, and I remembered how it felt to have a crew.

Anyway, back to the text messages.

I started to read them and I instantly regretted it.

[5:30 am] Harper: Um . . . is anyone awake?

[5:41 am] Harper: Still no one?

[5:43 am] Harper: I have some EXCITING news!

[5:57 am] Harper: Do you all have your phones on silent? What if this were an EMERGENCY!!!

[6:02 am] Harper: I'm not being dramatic. This actually IS kind of an emergency.

[6:11 am] Gus: For the love of weekends, Harper, what do you want

[6:14 am] Harper: Wellllll . . .

[6:44 am] Sophie: Harper, please respond. Gus just woke me up because he's worried you might've been abducted sometime in the past half hour. Or maybe you found a portal to another dimension?

[6:46 am] Gus: I'm just saying, it's rude to wake everyone up and then ghost us

[7:02 am] Harper: Sorry. Trying to decide the best way to break this to you . . .

[7:11 am] Sophie: Well, you officially have my attention

[7:20 am] Harper: Earth to Luke. That's me pounding on your wall. Wake up!

[7:25 am] Gus: Harper, I swear . . . I'm about to block your number

[7:28 am] Harper: OK OK OK

[7:29 am] Harper: Um

[7:30 am] Harper: It's just that we kind of . . .

[7:31 am] Harper: Sort of . . .

[7:32 am] Harper: Went viral? A little bit?

That was the end of the text chain.

But just the beginning of everything else.

★★★

"Harper June Gage-Flashman!" I yelled, stomping to my sister's door. I flung it open.

I found Harper upside down. Literally, she was doing a headstand in the middle of her jumbled floor, surrounded by clothes and costumes and makeup and *stuff*. I spotted her silver leotard-thing from the video sprawled across the floor, her favorite sweater dangling from her open dresser drawers, and some shiny piles of glitter all over the carpet. Multicolored markers and papers were strewn across the rainbow sheets on her unmade bed, and a tall pile of theater props teetered dangerously in the corner.

(Related: What kind of musical needs a painting of a dog's skeleton to move the story along?)

She fell over when I barged in.

"Ow," she said, rubbing her head.

"What is going on?" I demanded.

"Quiet!" she hissed, her eyes big. She pointed downstairs to where our moms were. I closed the door behind me and dropped my voice to a whisper.

"Explain."

She scoffed. "I mean, I think I explained it PRETTY WELL over text, Luke!"

I thrust my phone at her. In addition to all the texts, there were multiple missed video calls from Sophie and Gus. "You call this 'explaining'? How could we 'go viral' when we weren't online at all!"

"I said, be quiet!" Harper jumped up and placed the palm of her hand over my mouth. When she was positive I wouldn't yell anymore, she removed it and crossed her arms, staring at me accusingly. "When you're ready to talk CALMLY, I can fill you in."

I closed my eyes and used my tools. I took a deep breath, counted to ten, and exhaled.

That was better.

"Harper," I said again, slowly. "I'm going to tell Sophie and Gus to come over here right now, and you're going to talk."

In no time, I could see them walking over from next door—they didn't even knock when they arrived. They raced upstairs and closed the bedroom door tightly behind them. I couldn't tell what Gus was thinking—facial expressions are not my strength. But Sophie? That was easy. The anger radiating from her entire body was enough to cook a steak. Her eyes blazed, and her mouth was a sharp, straight line that cut across her face like a knife.

Not that I was looking at her closely, or anything like that. I'm just saying. I noticed.

The three of us crowded together in the middle of Harper's rug. I stepped on a stuffed elephant by mistake.

"Spill," Sophie demanded.

"So . . . well . . . let me start by saying I didn't MEAN to make us famous . . ." Harper's voice trailed off.

My stomach did a strange flip.

Sophie closed her eyes. Her words were tense. "Define *famous*."

Harper held up her phone. "Well, I kind of posted our video to Cre8."

I blinked at her screen while the words processed inside my brain. It was weird, how I could suddenly feel my heart beating, echoing in my ears and my skull. Was I having some kind of medical event?

"And it kind of took off overnight . . ." Harper shrugged, trying to keep the smile off her face. But of course she failed, because "taking off" is everything Harper has ever wanted.

"Define *took off*," Gus said.

Harper scrunched up her nose. Her voice got sort of tiny and breathy, like she was playing a character. "Like, over a hundred thousand views?" She glanced at her phone. "Actually, now it's three hundred thousand . . ."

We were all quiet for a moment, considering that. Outside, someone started a lawn mower. A bird sang. And all the noise in my brain, which I worked so hard to keep at a low volume, dialed itself up.

Sophie's face, normally a warm brown shade, turned a bit green. Her voice got all high and squeaky. "Three hundred thousand views?"

Harper blinked. "It's the *After Launch* tag I added to it. People are really loving that game!"

Sophie squeezed her eyes shut. "I repeat, *three hundred thousand views?*"

"Shhhh!" Harper said, her eyes darting to the door. She gestured to the hallway. "Do you all WANT to get CAUGHT?"

Sophie collapsed on Harper's bed. The fluffy yellow comforter enveloped her, and only the top of her brown hair was visible. "We're doomed."

"But . . . who . . . I mean, how . . . I . . ." I rubbed my eyes as if I could rub away the brain noise. I hadn't felt a roaring in my head like this in a while. "I'm so confused."

"To summarize," Gus said slowly. "It turns out, Harper has a secret Cre8 account. And she posted our video last night. And people like it?"

"LOVE it," Harper corrected.

"Harper!" Sophie cried, her voice still muffled from the blankets.

"I'm sorry," Harper muttered. Then she straightened up, lifted her chin. She crossed her arms defiantly across her chest. "No, you know what? I'm not sorry. In fact, YOU'RE WELCOME."

My hands felt weird. My toes, too. The back of my neck. All of my skin, actually. What was happening to me?

Was this what fame felt like?

Sophie sat up. "We're gonna be in so much trouble!" she said. "You have to delete it."

"But no one knows it's us!" Harper pointed out. "Let's just see what happens."

"What happens?!" Sophie repeated. She did a forward roll off the bed, landing on her feet in front of Harper. She was still in her plaid pajama pants and a pair of fuzzy slippers with yellow happy faces on them. I tried to focus on those slippers to help dull the sensory overload.

Sophie snapped, "Don't you get it? Nothing can happen! We have to take it down. Tell her, Gus!"

But Gus was kind of looking at the floor, kicking a pair of Harper's ballet slippers around, his hands in the pockets of his shorts. His hood was pulled up over his head, his shoulders slumped.

"Gus?" Sophie prompted.

He shrugged. "You can't even see our faces in the video. We're in costumes. And Harper's Cre8 account doesn't have her name or location or anything on it."

"Exactly!" Harper clasped her hands together, grinning. "So I guess I'm fine with just leaving it up."

Sophie gaped at her brother. Her mouth opened and I flinched, preparing for her fury. But just then, there was a fast knock at the door, and before we could answer, the knob turned.

Mom T's head popped in. She grinned.

"What's this, a meeting of some secret society?" she teased. "What are you all waiting for? Come down for pancakes!"

"Gimme a *P, A, N*—" Harper started to cheer. She stopped when Sophie shot her a glare so intense, I finally understood the phrase "if looks could kill." (Idioms can be tricky for me.)

"Be down in a minute," I said. "School project," I added, in case Mom T was wondering.

But that made Mom T get all excited. "Ooh, a group project? With the four of you? What's it about?"

My brain blanked.

I wish everyone else's had, too, but instead they all spoke at once.

"Dinosaurs!" Sophie barked.

"Taylor Swift!" Harper exclaimed.

"World War One!" Gus said.

Mom T squinted at us, confused.

I cleared my throat. "We're still trying to figure that part out."

"Ah." She shrugged. "Don't let the pancakes get cold!" she said, and then left.

"Dinosaurs?" Gus hissed. "What are we, in kindergarten?"

Sophie threw her hands up in the air, exasperated. "It's better than Taylor Swift!"

Harper gasped. "Nothing is better than Taylor Swift!"

My head started to throb. "Enough."

The cool thing about not talking a lot, I've learned, is that when you finally do talk, people usually listen. They all looked at me.

"The question is, do we delete the video or not, right?" I asked.

They nodded. "There's no deadline on our question. We don't have to decide right now. Let's think it over. We have all day to figure it out."

"Deal," Gus said quickly.

"Yay!" Harper agreed.

Sophie, our holdout, shook her head. To Harper, she said, "You promise you won't upload anything else there? Or leave a comment? Or —"

Harper held a hand over her heart. "Promise. I swear on my signed *Playbill* of *Wicked*."

Harper loved *Wicked*. Even Sophie looked impressed.

My stomach growled. "Come on. I'm *wicked* hungry."

They all groaned at my bad joke. But on the way downstairs, I'm pretty sure I saw Sophie smile. And that was something, at least.

CHAPTER FIVE
Sophie

Have you heard of the "Sunday Scaries"? It's that feeling some people get on Sundays, when the weekend is almost over and they're getting ready for school or work the next day. I've never had this problem. Maybe it sounds weird, but I like school! I always have. After all, what's not to like? All my friends are there, the vegan nuggets from the cafeteria are banging, and I don't have to hear the sound of a soccer ball constantly drumming against my bedroom wall.

Okay, fine, there's more about school that I like than just that stuff. For example, I've always been into math, and this year's Pre-Algebra has sort of blown my mind wide open. (Multiplying letters instead of numbers? I'm here for that.) And let's face it, school is basically the only place I see my brother these days.

It also helps that school is the one thing I positively, absolutely, can NOT quit. Like, legally. So, I look on the bright side.

That Sunday, though? The Scaries came for me. What if I walked into school tomorrow, and kids were talking about that video? What if they started to figure out that it was *us* who made it? And maybe they told our parents?

I couldn't sit still. I couldn't take a deep breath. I couldn't even pick up my phone, since I was so worried about what I'd find.

Gus, Harper, and even Luke seemed fine—excited, even. During breakfast, they devoured the pancakes, shooting each other looks when Luke and Harper's moms weren't watching. There was a buzz in the kitchen, is what I'm saying, and not the bumblebee kind. Meanwhile, I could barely eat one bite. My orange juice sat untouched, and my stomach felt like it had a flock of birds trapped inside, flapping their wings to get out.

Finally, when breakfast was over, the four of us had a chance to be alone again. I wasn't surprised when Gus led us all to the trampoline in our backyard. It had basically been the Rowan Roadies Headquarters, back in the day. Thanks to its netting and some large tree branches looming over it, the trampoline felt somewhat private. Cozy. Safe.

"What's the latest, Harp?" Gus asked, his voice low and urgent.

Harper studied her screen. "It's tripled since this morning. Nine hundred thousand and rising."

Gus whistled. "We'll be over a mill by lunch."

I glanced at the back door to make sure my parents were still out of earshot. I could see them through the sliding glass doors, hanging in the kitchen and making their usual Sunday shopping lists. Mom liked to unwind by cooking, and Dad liked to unwind by planning.

They would truly ground us for life if they knew what we'd done. It wasn't just that we'd broken the rules on Saturday night, but we'd blasted through all our technology rules, too!

See, my parents weren't exactly the "Go to your room!" kind of folks. They were usually very reasonable. But they did have some—well, let's call them *strongly held beliefs*—about the amount of time Gus and I spent on our phones and what we were, or were not, allowed to do with them. And while Gus and I had never been punished in any serious way, this would be a case where there would be consequences. Probably of the you'll-never-see-these-phones-again kind.

Even getting phones in the first place had been a hard-fought battle. In fact, we technically only *had* phones because Gus's soccer schedule meant we constantly needed to coordinate—and re-coordinate—family schedules. And when we got our phones, Harper and Luke got them, too. Our parents, as usual, coordinated on their rules.

Our phones were hand-me-downs and with cracks in the screens and lots of screentime limits. Randomly, a parent could ask to see our phones to do spot checks on what we were up to. But following all these rules was the price we paid for keeping up with our friends. And I guess the bonus was that the rules sort of forced us to stay out of the online drama middle schoolers were known for. I'd never *tell* my parents this, but part of me was grateful.

So . . . Cre8 was one of the platforms that was forbidden. I knew Luke didn't have an account there—he didn't have one anywhere, except for that one that let him game with people all over the world, which Mom B watched carefully. Harper, though? Who knew what rules she was sneaking around?

"Every second we waste wondering if we should delete it is another second we risk getting caught," I realized.

"Let's play this out," Harper suggested. "Hypothetically, say we get caught. So what?"

I couldn't believe my ears. "What—I mean—getting caught means—it's—we . . ."

The words felt so big, I couldn't get them out.

Luke cleared his throat. "First, we'd lose our phones. Second, we'd lose our parents' trust. And third, the kids at school would . . . like, know." He shuddered. "Which, for some of us, would be a good thing. But for me . . . *blech*."

"For me?" Harper twirled and struck a pose. "HEAVEN! That last part, anyway."

Gus looked unconvinced. He had to have an opinion, but he didn't say a word.

Losing my phone would be annoying. But having Mom and Dad lose trust in me? That would be *bad* bad. See, I didn't have the greatest track record when it came to my word. Every time I tried a new activity or sport or class, I would swear it was the one for me. That ever-elusive *thing*, like Gus and his soccer, that would become my defining hobby. I'd tried them all, and the only one that had any lasting impact was gymnastics. But even the thrill of occasionally flying upside down wasn't enough to make me commit to weekly classes. Now I just tumbled on my own, when the mood struck.

But once you think you've found your *thing* a few dozen times, people stop believing you. Even if you really, really mean it. Even if you really, really *want* it to be true.

And then . . . what Luke said about not being anonymous?

Valleyville Junior High isn't a huge place, but it's easy to feel overwhelmed by it, especially coming from the tiny elementary school we all went to. If our video kept getting shared, eventually someone at Valleyville Junior High would see it. But I'd learned that the best way to get through junior high was to avoid drawing attention to yourself, no matter what Harper might think.

My hand shot up in the air. "All those in favor of deleting it and forgetting this ever happened?"

But no one else raised their hand.

"Come on! Are you all serious?"

"Look," Luke said, and we all turned to him in surprise. I think Luke said more words to me that weekend than he had in the past three years combined. "I'm not ready to cast a vote yet, Sophie. I don't know what we're dealing with here. Does anyone outside of Cre8 even pay attention to what's on there? How big a risk is this anyway?"

"Great question," Harper said importantly, shifting her position and causing all of us to bounce up and down for a second. "Cre8 has about a quarter billion users, and most of it focuses on creative works. People dancing, singing, drawing, all of that. And yeah, there's some crossover to other social media sites, too. Cre8 is known for being a trendsetter, so our video will start popping up on other sites, too. Which means we'll get even MORE views!"

This was not exactly encouraging.

"How do you know so much about it?" Luke asked. "You're not even allowed to *be* on Cre8!"

Harper waved her hand, dismissing the idea. "Details!"

"Let's be real," I argued. "This video has to come down."

But Gus shrugged. "Does it, though? No one's gonna know it's us."

I screamed with my mouth closed. Then, for some reason, I turned to Luke. "Please give them a reality check!"

Harper jumped in before her brother could respond. "Not only should we not delete this one, but I think we should make more! We're MAGIC when we're together!"

"More?" I said. Did I hear that right?

"I'll do all the work," Harper offered. "By acting out other popular scenes from *After Launch*, we'll build a huge audience, *fast*. We'll become the biggest, most anonymous Cre8 stars around!"

This situation was taking on a life of its own.

"You're just saying that because you think it will, like, get you a movie deal," Luke said. "What about the rest of us?"

Harper sighed dramatically. "In case you hadn't noticed, I hope ANYTHING will get me a movie deal." Then her eyes lit up and she grinned at her brother. "Have I mentioned we could make actual money with this?"

Luke pushed his glasses up the bridge of his nose. "I'm listening."

"Sponsorships. Ads. You'd be able to buy all the video games you want."

Luke didn't respond, but he did cross his arms and lean back against the trampoline's netting. I was losing him!

I turned to Gus. "This is a bad idea, right?"

But Gus squinted at Harper. "You really think we could do this?"

She held a hand to her heart. "I do."

"But people will figure out it's us!" I reminded him.

"I don't think they will," Gus said, shrugging. "Our faces are completely covered."

I was struggling with my brother's reaction. It made no sense! "But . . . why? Why would you want to waste your time on this?"

Gus looked at his hands. Then the sky. Then the grass. Basically, at anything but me.

"I like *After Launch*," he finally said. "And writing skits about it sounds really fun, actually. I can think of ten video ideas off the top of my head that I'd love to write."

Before yesterday, I would have bet all the money in my piggy bank (which is really a bank in the shape of Wonder Woman) that Gus would demand to delete the video. He had way too much going on with soccer. But now? Clearly, I was mistaken.

Harper burst into applause. "Exactly, Gus! I knew you'd get it. Look at our soccer star, broadening his horizons!"

Gus looked uncomfortable. "I like other stuff."

"Food doesn't count," Luke, in a surprising move, joked. (It was weird, but I felt kind of proud of him?)

"I like other stuff *besides food*," Gus corrected himself. "And I can be just as creative as you guys can."

Harper pointed out the obvious. "It's just that you're kind of known for having a one-track mind."

In a flash, Gus jumped to his feet and began bouncing, which sent us all rolling around the trampoline.

"What, because I'm good at soccer, I can't try anything else?" He stopped bouncing and came out with his secret. "I actually just won the sixth-grade creative writing award."

"Whoa," Luke said.

"Incredible!" Harper cheered.

I'd thought he didn't want to tell anyone.

"We do all contain multitudes," Luke said, and while I didn't quite understand what that meant, I *did* understand that maybe I didn't know Gus as well as I thought I did.

Gus began jumping again, all around the perimeter of the trampoline. And sometimes, the only way to get Gus to talk was to meet him where he was. So I hopped up, too, and began following his jumping. Maybe I could convince him to change his mind . . . before we got ourselves caught up in something we couldn't stop.

When I got close enough that I didn't think Harper and Luke could overhear me, I whispered, "You really think this is a good idea?"

Gus abruptly stopped jumping. It made my knees buckle, and I collapsed onto the trampoline.

"Ow!" Harper said when I landed on her knee.

Gus stood over us, his hands on his hips. "I'm not saying it's a good idea. I'm saying it might not be a *bad* idea. But what about you, Soph? You could be our producer. You're bossy enough. So what's holding you back?"

I opened my mouth. I thought it was obvious: parents finding out, other kids finding out . . . basically, anyone finding out!

But the words wouldn't form. It was like they were glued in my throat.

Gus smirked. "Let me guess. Afraid of committing?"

Harper gasped dramatically, Luke's jaw dropped, and I stared, frozen, at my brother. Because he was right. And it didn't feel great to be called out like that in front of my old (and kind of new) friends.

I've quit every single thing I've ever tried—usually just about when I start to get good at it. It was probably what I was most known for. I didn't have the Sunday Scaries; I had the Stick-with-it Scaries.

I didn't know what to say, but I didn't have to say anything. Because just then, there was a rustling, followed by footsteps.

"Heya!"

"Argh!" Harper yelled. I jumped, too, my heart racing. Had we been caught? We all spun around to see who was there.

"Whatcha doing?" Olivia, our wannabe babysitter, asked. She strolled through our garden and started to climb up the trampoline ladder.

I stifled a groan.

"Look at you guys!" Olivia marveled. Her long dark hair was piled up in a giant ponytail at the top of her head, and she had a bunch of scratches down her arms from where she'd fallen off her bike the other night. She rubbed at them absentmindedly. "Hanging out together like the old days! Remember when I used to play teacher with you?"

"How could we forget?" Luke said. He'd never been a fan of Olivia—she was, if it was possible, even more high-strung than Harper. But yes, she used to pretend to be our teacher. She would lead us all around the neighborhood, calling us her students, and try to teach us long division.

"Well, it's cool to see you all together again," Olivia said, beaming. "Like old times!"

Why did she have to make it weird?

Because . . . it *was* kinda weird, right? I glanced around the trampoline. I lived with Gus, obviously, but we didn't exactly hang out together. And now here we were, spending the entire weekend in each other's presence.

"So, what's the occasion?" Olivia continued.

Gus laughed nervously. "What do you mean?"

Olivia shrugged. "You guys just look like you're up to something. Are you brainstorming for the Rowan Road block party?"

Our trampoline time was none of her business.

"Yeah, totally," I said. "The block party!"

Olivia nodded slowly, like she knew I was lying. No one said anything else, and eventually Gus started jumping again, aggressively enough that Olivia was forced to crawl back down the ladder. She narrowed her eyes at us.

"Okay, well, have fun with the 'block party,'" she said, using air quotes. She walked toward the side gate, which by the way she'd left open. What if Gus's pet turtle had been out here? Or Harper's cat?

When she finally disappeared, the four of us sort of stared at each other for a minute. Then I pointed at the fence.

"*That*," I declared. "That's what I'm worried about."

But Gus waved his hand. "She's just bored and trying to rile us up."

"I agree," Harper said. "Olivia's harmless. And I'm glad she stopped by—I'd forgotten the block party was almost here. We have to make this one extra good!"

"Why? Block parties are for little kids and old adults," Gus said.

"Period," added Luke.

Harper's jaw dropped. "*Hel-lo?* Didn't you hear? All four of our parents are in charge of this one."

We all looked blankly at her. "Does no one remember last year's DRAMA?" she continued.

Harper clapped her hands once, rubbed them together, and took a deep breath. Her eyes sparkled. "Okay. So. After we cleaned out the hot cocoa table in the first twenty minutes of last year's block party, and ate all the cotton candy before the little kids could get any? And after Gus's cleats popped a hole in the bounce house? And Luke kept unplugging the deejay's power cords because the music was too loud? Some of the neighbors were NOT pleased. Nancy from the red house up the hill accused our parents of, quote, never participating, and also, quote, of not contributing enough funds to make up for, and I quote again, the DEVASTATION. So our parents are all in charge of this year's, and I'm pretty sure Mom B is already writing a LONG list of rules for us. And we probably deserve it."

The memories flooded back. That block party had not been our finest moment.

Harper's glossy lips formed a grim line. "Word on the street is that our families nearly got banned from all future parties."

"How do you know all this gossip?" I asked. The only neighbors she hung out with were us . . . and not so much these days.

"People tell me things," she said a bit mysteriously.

We could circle back to the block party later. Right now, thousands of people were watching us on Cre8. We had to prioritize! "Luke?" I said. "What about you?"

He looked up from his phone, where his fingers had been frantically tapping the screen. He must've been playing some sort of game. I remembered that was one of the tools he used to help stay regulated (which was another way of saying "in control of his emotions and behavior"). "Me?"

"Yes, YOU." Harper nudged his shoulder. "What do you want to do with our video?"

Luke adjusted his glasses while considering the question. The birds above sang an entire song while we waited for his answer. He looked at everything around us except for our actual faces. Luke hated being put on the spot like this.

"And?" Harper prodded.

"And, I'm still not sure what my feelings are, so I don't want to say yet," he said.

Which was possibly the most sensible thing one of us had said all day.

But Harper clasped her hands together and batted her eyelashes. She wasn't letting her brother off the hook. "Come on, Luke! Let's be famous together!" she begged.

"Hang on. Why do you think another video would go as viral as this one anyway?" I said.

Harper protested. "It totally would! Once you have one viral video, you're a million times more likely to have another! That's just MATH."

Luke coughed. "That's inaccurate, Harp."

Gus looked smug. "But speaking of math, it's two against one right now. Two-point-five, if you count Luke."

"But . . ." I said. "But . . . we're not content creators, or whatever. We couldn't even make another good video if we tried!"

Harper's eyes sparkled. "Oh yeah?"

"Imagine what we'll come up with when we actually put in some effort," Gus said.

"Our videos will be AM-AAAAAZING!" Harper echoed.

"We're gonna be huge," Gus continued.

"Cre8's biggest stars!" Harper grinned.

I glanced at Luke. He wasn't as excited as Harper and Gus, but he was *not* miserable. I didn't understand. How could they all be so sure?

"I promise, Soph," Harper said, as if she could read my mind. "Our dreams are about to come true!"

Harper's dreams, maybe.

Which got me wondering . . . what even *were* my dreams?

And if this was *their* dream, why weren't they terrified of failing?

Which gave me an idea. Because I was pretty used to trying new things and discovering they were harder than I thought.

I bounced as high as I possibly could and then executed a flawless front tuck. Yes, I was flipping out!

I would call their bluff!

When I landed, breathless, I stuck out my hand. "Let's try one more video."

"Woo-hoo!" they cheered. Even Luke, which surprised me.

I held up a hand. "But."

"Uh-oh." Harper stopped cheering.

"If it isn't as popular as this one, we don't do any more. In fact," I declared, "if our second video doesn't surpass the first one in views, we'll delete the entire Cre8 account."

Then they'd see how it felt to fail.

I stuck out my hand. "Deal?"

Harper was the first to shake. "Girl, you got a deal. I can't wait to prove you wrong."

Gus was next. "You have no idea what you're getting yourself into."

Finally, Luke's hand landed on top of ours. "Sophie, you're something else."

I didn't blush, exactly; it was just really warm out all of a sudden. We managed some kind of silly four-way shake.

It was *on*.

MermaidGirl_333: Dude this is funny, do another? [48,543 Likes]

11FindMeOnTwitch11: I'm a gamer snob and kinda think this video is even cooler than the game, NGL [104,111 Likes]

Yo_itsSmitty: Are those Ghostbusters costumes? Genius [1,989 Likes]

TheHarbourTriplets: WHO YOU GONNA CALL, THE LORGANS [23,709 Likes]

JusticeWarrior17: Tagging all my #afterlaunch friends did y'all see this? @hollymac1 @jjjindahomie @AfterLaunchFan999 [33 Likes]

MaddielovesAbe: More! Do another one! [987 Likes]

OliviatheQueena: Is it just me or is there something SO familiar about this video? [4 Likes]

CHAPTER SIX
Gus

Screech!

The whistle blew. My head hanging, ashamed, I jogged over to the sidelines.

One of my teammates, Austen, slapped me on the shoulder. "Come on, Gus!"

"Dude," said Colton, Valleyville's goalie. "Get your head in the game!"

"Chill out," I mumbled. I chugged some water and then poured it over my face, which was slick with sweat and studded with dead bugs that had found themselves in my path while I was trying to score. My stomach growled. "It's just a scrimmage."

"Just?" Colton said.

"Who are you and what did you do with Gus Magee?" Austen joked.

But I was not in a joking mood. That day at school had been like walking a tightrope, trying to be my normal self while also avoiding any talk of the hottest viral video. In fact, I'd started pretending I hadn't heard of *After Launch* the *game*, let alone the video—*our* video—now that it had finally landed in my friends' feeds.

Yeah. Suddenly it seemed like *every*one at Valleyville Junior High had seen our video at the same time. It started when I was walking to homeroom . . .

"Yo, Magee!"

Even in all the laughter and shouting and gossip ringing through the hallways, Diego Pratt's voice stuck out. So did his head, since he was at least a half foot taller than any other kid. Since Diego is basically the hero of the eighth grade, I was surprised to be singled out.

"Hey, bro," I said, slapping his palm. He was with his girlfriend, this other eighth grader named Claire Fitzpatrick, but she was on her phone and barely even looked at me.

Until.

Diego had just asked me "How's it hanging," and I was looking for the perfect response, only my brain was blanking because I couldn't figure out why Diego Pratt was talking to me at all, when Claire saved the day.

"Have you guys seen this? It's *so* sigma!" She held up her phone and blew a bubble with her gum. Diego and I both peered at her screen, but I knew already. I just had this feeling. I didn't even need to look at her phone.

She was watching our *After Launch* video.

"Dude!" Diego burst into laughter. "Of course I saw it, I'm the one who sent it to you! Magee, you gotta watch."

I forced a smile. "Yeah, I saw it, uh, last night. Funny stuff."

"Funny? It's genius!" Claire began dancing like the Lorgans. Or like Harper, technically. Which was weird to see! I quickly averted my eyes.

"Anyway, Magee, I wanted to tell you—I heard you're the sixth-grade winner of the school writing award?" Diego nodded and pointed proudly to himself. "I'm the eighth-grade winner. I'll see you at the writing camp this summer?"

I froze. How did Diego Pratt know I had won the writing award?

Luckily, the bell rang and saved my butt. Diego just held his hand up for another high five, Claire snapped her gum, and off they went, swallowed by the hallway crowds.

If Diego Pratt knew, who else did? What about Coach? What about my parents?

I had bigger problems just then, though. As I hustled to homeroom, I passed another group of kids replaying the video on someone's phone about four hundred times, the bleeping noises of the alien soundtrack Luke had laid over our video echoing over and over, until one of the science teachers begged them to put their devices away and get to class.

And then, when I finally made it to my seat, eager for the morning announcements for the first time in history, I noticed something unusual.

Harper and I had homeroom together, but I always sat with some of the guys from soccer in the back corner of the room, while she sat with the theater kids up front, right next to our homeroom teacher's desk. (That would be Mr. Ouma, the assistant drama coach.) Sometimes Harper and I would catch each other's eyes and wave, but that was pretty much the extent of our in-school communication.

That morning, though, when I slipped into my seat and pulled up my hood to have a couple seconds of peace—there's something about the way a hoodie can block out the rest of the world, you know?—I felt Harper staring at me. I shot her a questioning glance, then she widened her eyes and gestured to her friends. As far as I could tell, her friends were doing what theater kids do: practicing lines, goofing around, being loud. But I couldn't figure out what Harper was trying to say, and with Colton chattering away about our next scrimmage, soon I couldn't focus on her at all.

Until she coughed a loud, fake cough.

How did I know it was fake?

Because she barked it in my direction and then glared meaningfully at me.

Could she *be* any more obvious?

I was about to go see what she wanted when her friend Aria Moore—who by the way Colton definitely had a crush on, even though he would never admit it—leaped to her feet and then jumped onto a chair!

"Everyone, do the Lorgan dance!" she cried. She began waving her arms and circling her neck, mimicking exactly what Harper had done in our video.

Oh. That's what Harper had been trying to tell me—that her friends were just as obsessed with our video as everyone else. If I had to choose one word to explain the look on Harper's face, it would be *proud*.

Almost immediately, the theater kids followed Aria's lead, jumping to their feet and dancing around the front of the room. Then, to my utter shock, Mr. Ouma joined them.

"Lor-gans! Lor-gans!" Someone started a chant, and soon our whole homeroom class was in on it.

Except for me. And Harper.

Which we both realized—at exactly the same time—was pretty fishy. Because if anyone had noticed, they might've been able to put two and two together and come up with four Rowan Roadies.

So Harper also got out of her seat and began dancing and singing, and generally reenacting the very video she'd created. The problem was that she looked a little too much like the Lorgan in the video . . .

Thank goodness Harper is an actor. She could always blame the similarity on her talent. Still . . . it was an out-of-body experience. A real mind game.

Which probably explains why, at the scrimmage later that day, I got absolutely pummeled on the field. I couldn't get it together, and my teammates noticed.

"Great job out there, man," Colton said sarcastically after I'd failed to steal the ball—twice. Coach blew the whistle and the team gathered around the sidelines to wait for his pep talk. "Your parents should get a refund for all that private coaching."

I thwacked my jersey at him. "Shut up, bro. We're all allowed to have bad days."

Austen whistled. "We mortals are, but Gus Magee has *never* had a bad soccer day."

Maybe Austen had a point. Not to brag, but I was a consistently strong player, and yeah, I felt really crappy about how I let the team down today. I wasn't used to that. But why couldn't these guys give me a break?

Coach came walking toward us, all business.

"Magee!" he called. His voice was sharp, and Coach was usually a reasonable guy, but I'd really messed up out there.

His silver sunglasses had such dark lenses that I couldn't see his eyes, but you know how you can feel when someone is annoyed with you? That feeling definitely came through. "Magee, take a break. Use this time to figure out where you put all those skills I know you have."

Ouch.

He blew the whistle, and the team ran back to the field. On the bench, I jiggled my knees and watched my teammates try to salvage the mess I'd made while I inhaled a couple of granola bars I had stashed behind the water cooler.

After a few minutes, Coach approached me.

"Did you find 'em?" he asked, arms crossed, whistle hanging around his neck. With those sunglasses and his gray windbreaker and matching sneakers, his whole vibe was giving human-alien hybrid . . . like some kind of Lorgan.

Actually, that gave me an idea. In my English class, we were studying short stories, and we were supposed to write our own stories based on something found in nature. Yawn, right? Everyone was probably going to write about their pets, or something cheesy about full moons and stars.

But what if I wrote about an alien that crash-lands in a forest and creeps around a small town at night, and—

"Magee!"

I jumped. "Uh, no. I mean, yes! Yes, I found my missing skills." I straightened up and tried to show him I was ready to play, not hungry and not distracted. I tried to show him I was only thinking about soccer.

He eyed me for a long minute. Or at least I think he was eyeing me. Again, it was hard to tell with those shiny sunglasses.

"Get out there and do your best."

I jumped up, dashing over to my spot on the field. And for a while, I was back to myself: Gus Magee, soccer star. In the first three minutes, I scored a goal and assisted in another. My feet dodged and twisted and jumped at all the right times. I could practically feel Coach's icy attitude thawing.

But then I glanced at him, and at those sunglasses, and thought, *Lorgan!*

And of course that made me think of our video.

I wasn't into being famous, exactly, the way Harper was. Being anonymous was fine with me! But I kept thinking about how great it would be to write a script, to see how creative I could be. I liked the idea of making our next video better than the first one—and proving my sister wrong in the process.

Whoosh!

The unmistakable sound of a soccer ball landing in a net echoed over the field.

"*Magee!*"

In a flash, I realized the ball I had been dribbling as I made my way down the field had been stolen from me by the opposing team, and that noise had been *their* winning goal soaring into the net.

As for me? I'd been kicking nothing but air for a solid ten seconds.

★★★

I trudged home with my head in my hands. Metaphorically. Though it did feel extra heavy, what with everything I had on my mind.

Coach sometimes made us watch videos of our games to see where we could improve. Lots of our parents would text clips of us playing, too, so we got to see different angles. I guessed this was one of those days where I would need to watch every clip I could find. Maybe I could figure out where I'd lost my magic.

But studying my game felt like . . . well, studying.

And didn't I already do enough of that?

Shouldn't the sport I loved be more fun? I was just a kid, after all.

The closer I got to home, the farther away soccer started to feel. And as I hiked up Rowan Road, my house in sight, I got a rush of excitement so fierce, I almost thought I'd start flying. Here at home, I was free to start thinking about our next video.

I didn't know if what I was feeling was normal. To be so completely consumed by one passion for so long, only to suddenly have another, newer one take over. Writing was new and shiny, and soccer felt a little crusty. Old.

Well, I pushed *that* concerning thought out of my head—no time for self-reflection today!—and got back to daydreaming *After*

Launch–themed ideas for Cre8. When I reached my front door, I grabbed my phone and shot off a text.

> [4:49 pm] Gus: Meet on the trampoline in 5, urgent
>
> [4:50 pm] Harper: OOOOOOH THIS FEELS SO SECRETIVE!
>
> [4:51 pm] Luke: All caps, Harp? Really?
>
> [4:52 pm] Harper: 😒
>
> [4:54 pm] Sophie: Btw it's been 5 mins, you're all late

"So here's the deal," I said once everyone had gathered on the trampoline. "I know what I want to get out of this next video. I want to write the full script, from start to finish. But you all probably have your own goals. Yeah?"

Harper waved her hand in the air. "Should I outline my five-, ten-, and fifteen-year plans and how this fits into them? I have a slide deck AT THE READY!"

"We probably don't have time for that," I said.

"I think we all know your goals," Luke said dryly.

"Luke, what about you?" I asked.

He cleared his throat. "Well, I love gaming, obviously. So just having fun with *After Launch* is a goal of mine. But also, this gives me the chance to learn some of the newest design and effects software I've been reading about."

I nodded. "Nice. Soph?"

She hesitated. "Is it mean if I say that it's to prove that we'll never go viral again?"

"Not mean at all," Luke said. "Statistically likely, actually, no matter what Harper thinks."

"And," she said, pointing at all of us. "We all have a goal of not getting caught!"

"Bingo!" I said. "That's why we need some ground rules."

"Boo! Rules!" Harper said. She was eating a snack bag–sized bag of M&M's and she threw one into her mouth.

I stole an M&M from Harper and flipped open the notebook I'd used to jot down my thoughts earlier. I did a final scan of the surrounding yards to make sure no one else was within earshot.

"Coast clear," Luke assured me. He held up his phone to show us the screen. "I had some extra cameras hanging around, so I installed a couple. It was pretty easy. Now we can see all angles of both our houses." A pained look crossed his face. "Except for the far side of your house, Gus and Sophie. But there's no entry point that way, so I'm sure it's fine."

"Wow." I blinked. "Okay, cool; thanks, Luke. Anyway . . ."

I held up my list and began counting off my proposed rules. "The first thing we all need to swear to is, obviously, that no one else can know about this. We're not supposed to be on Cre8 at all, and if we get caught, our parents will . . ."

Sophie raised her hand. "Never trust us again?"

Harper shrugged. "Cancel my private acting lessons?"

Luke frowned. "Take away my Switch?"

"All of those things," I confirmed with a nod. "That means no one. Not 'no one except for my best friends.' So, Soph, you can't tell Jazzy. Harper, you can't tell your gaggle of fans. And, Luke . . ."

He shrugged. "No worries."

"Cool." I nodded. I had always sort of envied Luke's loner tendencies. Imagine being able to live your life without the weight of other people's expectations.

"I'm fine with that," Sophie confirmed. Harper pursed her lips but then nodded.

"Next, our username." I shot Harper a look. "PaDoodleCaboodle is, like, really obvious, Harp."

She mocked outrage. "Don't you dare bring my precious cat Poodle into this!"

Sophie rolled her eyes. "We're only filming one more video. Does it really matter?"

"Says you," Harper shot back.

We all fell silent. Finally, Luke spoke up. "How about 'HumansVsLorgans'?"

Harper squealed. "Perfect! It tells the user exactly what to expect: videos about *After Launch*. That'll get us noticed even more!"

Sophie frowned but didn't object. I shrugged. "Good with me."

"Nice," Luke said. He was trying to play it cool, but I knew that tone of voice. He was happy.

"Finally, safety." I pointed to Luke's phone. "This guy gets it. Luke's already thinking two steps ahead, with his security cameras. But we all need to be safety minded. And that means . . ."

I dramatically flipped over the next page in my notebook. I had drawn a chart that looked like this:

	Mom T	Mom B	Mom Magee	Dad Magee
Time In				
Time Out				
Location				
Observer				

Harper guffawed. "What is THAT!"

I was pretty proud of this, actually, despite Harper's snort, so I rushed to explain. "This is our Parent Tracking System."

Sophie's eyebrows shot up. "Our what now?"

"Our PTS. It's how we'll track where our parents are at any given time, so they don't catch us in costume or anything." I wondered if they had seen the video themselves.

"Let me see that," Luke demanded. He peered through his glasses as he studied it for a moment, and then nodded. "Yep. I can work with this. I'll convert it into an app."

"I still don't get it," Sophie groaned.

Just then, across the yard, the back door slid open. "Hi, kids!"

It was Dad, carrying a tray of food. He headed to the grill on the far side of the deck.

Mom and Dad had invited the Gage-Flashmans over for

dinner—just like old times. The eight of us used to eat together a couple times a week, alternating houses or back decks, grilling or even just ordering pizzas. But this was the first time our families had done this in a long time.

One time my mom told me about "friendship breaks." It's this idea that sometimes you drift close and then far and then close again to someone, but that you keep your bond with them no matter what. She stressed that years of friendship history were worth holding on to, even during a break. These friendships still hold up over time, as long as there's true respect and understanding on both sides.

From the trampoline, I watched Brynn and Tara open *their* back door, too, arms filled with salad bowls and hot dog buns and pitchers of iced tea, crossing their yard and setting the table on our deck.

Our parents had figured out how to ride those ebbs and flows, right? I glanced at Luke and Harper. Was that what we were doing, right now?

Whatever it was, it felt okay.

But I could also swear the sizzle of the grill was calling my name—*Gusssssss*—so I returned to the chart and dropped my voice to a whisper. "So, quickly: We'll each be responsible for identifying and tracking where our parents are at any given time. So, say I'm assigned to my dad right now; I'll log his movements on the chart—"

"In the app," Luke corrected. "Soon."

"Right, sure, in the app, so that we all always know where each of our parents is. And when we can see that they're all safe and accounted for—"

"In other words, out of the house for an extended period of time," Harper added, her eyes darting to her moms, who were pouring iced teas and dumping bags of salad.

"That's a green light to film a new video," I concluded.

"I'll build a green light push notification into the app every time all four parents are tracked in a location that's at least fifteen minutes away," Luke said.

"Burger time!" Dad's voice sailed across the lawn. "Hot dogs for everyone! Winner winner chicken dinner!"

Sophie groaned. *"Parents."*

Dad flipped the burgers and called over his shoulder, "I heard that!"

So we all crawled off the trampoline, put on our shoes, and ran up the deck stairs. (Well, three of us ran. Sophie tripped. She had on that sky-high pair of platform boots Harper had talked her into wearing, and she couldn't really walk in them.)

Have you ever tried to finish planning a top secret mission that your parents absolutely, positively can NOT find out about, while you eat potato salad right next to them? I don't recommend it.

Our four parents ate at the big round patio table, and we four kids squished onto the rickety old picnic table in the corner of the deck. My dad had been telling my mom he'd get rid of it for years, but I was glad he hadn't. Because this felt like old times. Dad passed over a tower of burger patties and everything else, like the rules and the videos and Coach's disappointment, just faded away. I pulled a splinter out of my shorts, squirted a glob of ketchup on my burger, and realized that, if this is what Cre8 would bring me, I would take it.

Then, when I was on my second hot dog (and, okay, my third helping of mac and cheese), Harper leaned in close and dropped her voice.

"We're gonna prove Sophie wrong, right?"

I kept chewing. Mom's mac and cheese was *killer* tonight, but part of me was also wondering what was for dessert.

Harper elbowed me.

"Right," I muttered.

Across the table, Sophie smirked like she had already won the bet. I grinned back, big and wide and showing all my teeth . . . plus the cheesy noodles I still had in my mouth.

"Ew!" she yelled. *"Mo-om!"*

But I just laughed. Sophie was so easy to psych out. This video challenge would be a piece of cake!

Mmm . . . *cake.*

CHAPTER SEVEN
Harper

Want to hear a secret?

I may LOOK like the most outgoing, confident kid at Valleyville Junior High.

But inside? I'm just making it up as I go along.

It's called ACTING.

And I sure needed to use those make-believe skills that week, when no one at school could stop gushing about the mega-viral *After Launch* role-playing video on Cre8.

Our video was EVERYWHERE. Every corner I turned, every hallway I passed, there was someone watching it on their phone. I mean, didn't we all have CLASSES to take and HOMEWORK to do? That first day, in homeroom, Gus and I had both been accosted by kids who couldn't stop acting it out. My drama friends point-blank asked me what I thought of it, and I forced myself to say, "Why, NO, I haven't heard about that viral Cre8 sensation! I'm totally out of the loop! Tell me everything!"

Pretending to have no knowledge of the hottest video around when you're known for being a trendsetter? An IMPOSSIBLE DILEMMA.

But at least they all believed me. Because while I might've been the person who posted our video, I *definitely* wasn't going to be the one who spilled the beans.

So there I was that Wednesday afternoon, sitting in the darkened Valleyville Junior High auditorium, pinching the skin on my knees to keep the grin off my face as our theater director, Ms. Hopper, took the stage. Who knew secrets could be so DELICIOUS? This one tasted like strawberry bubble gum.

She clapped her hands. "Attention, middle schoolers! Welcome to tryout week!"

I couldn't help it—I put down the bottle of root beer I'd been chugging and started clapping my hands so hard, they hurt. Naturally, everyone around me followed my lead.

I'd been so thrilled when the spring musical had been announced. I'd gone through an intense princess phase when I was little, and starring as Belle in *Beauty and the Beast Jr.* was going to really help me make my mark in the Valleyville theater community!

Plus . . . the COSTUMES!

I just had to GET the role first.

Ms. Hopper held up both hands in a *stop* signal. A single spotlight shone on her, and her wispy red hair floated around her big forehead (no offense, Ms. Hopper) and made her big green eyes shine. She looked nearly as excited as I felt.

And boy—did I ever feel excited! I was just a lowly sixth grader, and the spring musical was the first school production I was eligible to audition for. (We sixth graders had all been assigned to crew positions for the fall show. Can you imagine? ME, being backstage?!) No wonder the show was so lackluster.)

For a moment, I lost myself to my daydream, the one where I scored the lead role, with Selvi Gill as my understudy's understudy. (Was that even a thing? I wasn't sure! In my daydream, it made sense.)

"Opening night is just three months away, and soon we will choose our cast," Ms. Hopper continued. "Today, you'll each take the stage solo to show us what you've got!"

She nodded toward Mr. Ouma, her codirector. He waved at all of us. We whooped and cheered. The energy in the auditorium was electric!

Flanking me in the second row, front and center, were my closest pals, Aria Moore and Lila Vasquez. The hard truth about acting is that your BEST FRIENDS are often your BIGGEST COMPETITION— at least, when it comes to auditioning. But luckily, I didn't really have to worry about that. Aria was a gorgeous singer but couldn't act to save her life, and Lila gave off "best supporting actress" vibes—both onstage and off. Which, if I really thought about it, is probably why we were such great friends.

While I felt pretty confident about my ability to beat the other sixth graders, the seventh and eighth graders were a bigger challenge. They had more experience onstage than me, just since they were older. But I'd been tracking their successes closely over the years, and I knew I was a better performer than even Hailey Baker and Sloane Taank, last year's leads. I knew I had a solid shot at Belle! Though I would take Mrs. Potts, the other main female lead, if I needed to.

Suddenly, Ms. Hopper was off the stage, her clipboard on her lap, taking her position in the center of the first row, next to Mr. O.

Somehow, I had zoned out completely while Ms. Hopper was reading out the audition order. Frantic, I leaned over to Aria.

"I missed what she said! Who's up first?" I whispered.

But I shouldn't have even bothered asking, because by the time I did, Selvi Gill popped up from her spot in the third row. She strode to the stage, her head held high.

I hated to admit it, but Selvi looked incredible . . . like a STAR. She wore a sparkly red pleated skirt, a pink T-shirt with hearts all over it, and a thick, fuzzy pink headband that made her black hair look even more social media–ready than usual. On her feet? PINK PLATFORM SNEAKERS with SILVER STARS dotting them.

No one could take their eyes off Selvi. Including me.

Selvi and I had a complicated relationship. She was in sixth grade, too, and had a reputation for being perfectly nice to everyone, at all times. And perfectly prepared for every test. Her hair was always styled and her highlighter hugged her cheekbones just so. Her clothes never rumpled, as if she'd stepped out of the old-fashioned catalogs my moms still got in the mail. Everyone liked Selvi, as far as I could tell, though she was a bit of a loner. In fact, right there in the auditorium, while the rest of us were grouped with our besties in little pockets of seats, Selvi sat alone.

Maybe, in another world, Selvi and I would've been friends. But in this world, where only one person could play Belle?

We were MORTAL ENEMIES.

As she took the stage and awaited Mr. O's signal to begin, I began to fume. How DARE Selvi Gill show me up! She knew I loved bright colors! She knew hearts were my SIGNATURE LOOK!

Today I was wearing something a little more toned down than usual: black-and-white zebra-print leggings, a glittery purple tank top, and a striped orange-and-navy chunky cardigan. My hair was up in a ballerina bun and I wore my long silver earrings, the ones that made pretty tinkling noises whenever I moved my head. I'd even put on lip gloss!

I squeezed hands with Aria and Lila.

"This should be good," Lila breathed. I frowned.

Onstage, Selvi cleared her throat. "Hello. I'm Selvi Gill, and for my audition, I'll be reciting a monologue from Lumiere, the candelabra."

As she blinked in the spotlight, I held my breath.

The thing about spiraling is that you can do it very QUIETLY, so no one notices.

Then again . . . what is the POINT of spiraling if no one notices?

I pondered that question while I watched Selvi knock everyone's socks off with her audition. (Even Lila, who famously never wore socks, because she said the stitching on the toe part bothered her too much.)

And after I finished spiraling, I pouted.

It wasn't FAIR that Selvi Gill had gotten so good at acting! Acting was MY thing!

As she proudly walked offstage, I slumped in my seat. My mind raced. Was MY audition going to be good enough? Would people applaud for me like they did for her? Worse yet . . . what if I'd LOST MY MAGIC? My sparkle? My "it" factor???

My spiral was interrupted by my phone vibrating. I sneaked a glance, turning my screen's brightness down so it wouldn't be totally obvious in the dark auditorium.

[3:31 pm] Sophie: Wow, our video is still going viral! Still think the next one will top it? Or are you ready to admit there's no way you can win this bet?

[3:32 pm] Gus: You know I don't back down from a little challenge

[3:33 pm] Luke: You guys got the link for the PTS app I texted earlier, right?

[3:34 pm] Sophie: Yep—I already added Mom's details. Gus, you do Dad.

[3:35 pm] Gus: Stop bossing me around

[3:36 pm] Gus: OK done

[3:37 pm] Luke: The PTS says Thursday at 7 works. Let's film then?

[3:41 pm] Gus: Let's do it

[3:42 pm] Sophie: ☺

[3:43 pm] Gus: Can't wait to win

[3:45 pm] Harper: I am very busy trying to FOCUS on my AUDITION please stop texting so much

[3:45 pm] Harper: (Also Thursday at 7 is perfect, I'll text everyone my ideas tonight!)

[3:46 pm] Gus: No need. Already wrote something amazing.

[3:50 pm] Luke: Break a leg Harp

[3:51 pm] Sophie: Woohoo Harper! You got this!

[3:51 pm] Gus: We're all rooting for you!

[3:52 pm] Harper: 😊

I tucked my phone away. My cheeks hurt from grinning. How did the Rowan Roadies know I needed a pick-me-up at that VERY MOMENT? How MINDFUL AND DEMURE was it that they remembered I had my big audition?

Hmmmmmm, I said to myself. These texts reminded me that I had something Selvi Gill didn't have.

A VIRAL VIDEO.

Fame.

Fortune!

(Okay, no fortune yet. I reminded myself to research when it made sense to monetize our channel.)

But still—look at what I had accomplished already. Me, Harper June Gage-Flashman! The Cre8 sensation! Take THAT, Selvi Gill!

"Harper? Harper Gage-Flashman?"

Aria and Lila elbowed me. Ms. Hopper was peering into the

darkened theater, calling my name. I took a deep breath and rose slowly, so all eyes would be on me.

"Present," I said in my most mature voice.

Ms. Hopper seemed to choke back a laugh. "Okay, great, Harper. Ready for your audition?"

I lifted my chin. "Absolutely."

Then I made my way as elegantly as possible to the stage (which is DIFFICULT when you have to move through a row filled with people, tripping over their giant backpacks on the floor, but I think I handled it nicely) and climbed up the steps. With every step my confidence grew.

My sparkle was BACK!

I leaned into the warmth of the spotlight and adjusted the microphone. I couldn't see anyone, of course, because of the lights, but I could FEEL them.

I opened my mouth, ready to introduce myself—as if I NEEDED an introduction!

But instead of saying "Hello, I'm Harper, and I'll be performing Belle's bookstore scene," out came something else.

A massive, earth-shattering BURP.

Darn that root beer!

CHAPTER EIGHT
Luke

I'm good at focusing. Sometimes too good. Sometimes so-focused-I-forget-to-sleep-or-eat.

Which has its perks—don't get me wrong. It's how I was able to rebuild an old laptop I'd found in the basement in just one weekend. And how it took me just one week to beat the first game I'd ever played, the one that got me hooked on gaming.

And now? My ability to focus had paid off yet again. I'd spent the night mapping out exactly how to film our next video, and where, and when, and using which props. I'd sorted out which video editor offered the best special effects and figured out how to score a free trial of it.

Maybe even more important, I'd really thought about what we needed to accomplish. Our first video had taken off, and I wanted our second one to do even better. Because what's the point of doing anything again if you're not trying to improve? I might not be an expert at Cre8, but I figured being a content creator was probably similar to being a video game designer. You needed a great story to bring people back, characters who people could relate to, and production values that were always amping up.

You also needed the right equipment. I didn't quite have that yet—top-of-the-line cameras and software cost money, and it wasn't like I could ask my moms for any without explaining why I needed it. So we would have to make do.

I did this all on just three hours of sleep, a single protein bar, and the rest of Mom B's favorite orange juice.

The Rowan Roadies, and our next *After Launch* video, were ready. Or so I thought.

★★★

The plan was this: We would film a scene from one of the game's earlier challenges, where the Lorgans attack the humans outside the ship, floating in space. I'd had a blast playing this scene, and I'd found the perfect visual effects to make it seem real, but still like we were just some kids creating this. Because we were!

Gus had written a wacky script where Lorgan Sophie had to do some serious tumbling moves to block me and Gus (as astronauts) from getting back inside our ship, while Harper got to continue performing her signature (sort of) dance moves.

I'd planned so meticulously. So how come everything was falling apart?

"This app isn't working!" I groaned. It was Thursday, approximately 7:37 at night, and we were in Gus and Sophie's basement again, and my brain was that horrible combination of too wired *and* too tired.

"Is there something else we can use?" Sophie wondered.

"Sure, but it costs a ton of money," I snapped.

"Here, let me —"

"Come on!" I huffed, interrupting her. I didn't mean to be rude, and I hoped she remembered that sometimes, when I was really in my head about something, I'd forget that people were just trying to help. As the software failed to connect from my phone to the big screen I'd set up, I pounded the back of it in a fit of exasperation, then ripped out the cord and blew on it.

"Okay, Grandma," Harper muttered.

I sighed. I took a breath and reset, because Harper had a point. My grandma acted like technology that wasn't working just needed a little kick, like a vending machine whose Doritos got caught on the coil.

"Can we hurry it up a little?" Gus suggested, his voice muffled. He was in full costume, including the new helmet we'd constructed for our space suits. Technically, we needed a spheroidal dome helmet, but finding a realistic dupe was too expensive, and everyone was getting tired of me being so specific about it. "I'm dying in here!"

"I'm doing the best I can," I protested. "This stupid thing just isn't—"

Sophie gently pulled the phone from my hands. "Take five, Luke."

I watched as she tapped a few times on the screen, muttering something about my settings being messed up. To my complete surprise, within seconds my phone screen flashed up on the monitor I'd been trying to connect it to.

She handed it back to me, a smug smile on her face. "All set."

I blinked at her in awe. The Sophie I knew never remembered to *charge* her devices, let alone solve problems with them.

It felt kind of funny to learn something new about a person I'd known for so long.

Funny *nice*, not funny *funny*.

Gus clapped his hands together. In his astronaut costume, his hands were covered, and his mittens made a muted, soft noise that reminded me of snow. Between the noise and his white suit, which despite Harper's best costuming efforts still kind of resembled someone preparing to walk through a blizzard, I was hit with a sudden memory.

So many times as kids, the four of us had gotten all bundled up on snow days, wrapped in snowsuits and scarves and mittens, to climb up the hill of Rowan Road so we could sled down the icy, hushed streets. One of those times, when I was probably seven or eight, the storm had been super icy; Sophie and I, sharing a two-person sled, had trouble making it go the way we wanted. We careened down the hill, frozen with exhilaration as we passed our houses, where Sophie's dad was waiting for us. But the sled kept going, beyond the foot of the hill, until we actually crossed Main Street—luckily, it was deserted—and landed, breathless, in the bushes on the other side. We crashed so hard that we disturbed a ton of fresh snow in the trees above, and it fell down in such a rush that for a moment we couldn't see.

It almost felt like Sophie and I were the only people left in the world for a moment. And right then, I'd thought, *If there's anyone on the planet I'd want to be stuck alone with, it's Sophie.*

I hadn't thought of that memory in a long time.

The muffled clapping from Gus brought me back to reality. For reasons I couldn't explain, I avoided Sophie's eyes.

"Let's do this, then!" Harper cheered. "Are we ready?"

I sighed.

Because, actually, we weren't ready. At least not as ready as I thought we needed to be. Things were taking way too long, and nothing was going right. And when things don't go as I plan, I have trouble seeing past my mistakes.

For starters, according to our PTS, the Magees had reservations at the fanciest restaurant in Valleyville at 7:15. But they hadn't left the house until 7:19, which meant we started with a twenty-minute deficit. Considering my own moms were due home shortly after eight, we truly had just a few minutes to get this done.

But did anyone else understand that? No. They did not. So I would have to make them.

"Places, everyone," I reminded them. "We're running out of time."

Harper stomped to her spot. She was in a foul mood, thanks to her audition. All afternoon, she'd talked about the Burp That Nearly Destroyed Her.

"Coming," Sophie muttered, trying to catch up to Harper. But she couldn't move quickly; she was stumbling all over the place. I glanced down at her feet. I pointed.

"What are those?"

Sophie sighed as Gus and Harper looked down, too. Gus started cracking up.

"Oh hush," Harper said loftily. "It's called FASHION."

But Harper's encouragement didn't seem to make Sophie feel any better. She put her hands on her hips, about to retort with something snarky, but the movement made her wobble.

"It's giving kid-playing-dress-up," Gus said, shaking his head. "You can barely even walk!"

"I was just trying them out," Sophie explained. "You don't get it!" Curious, I peered through the camera. "Huh," I remarked. Sophie's newfound height, however shaky, *did* make it easier to capture us all in the same frame. But I couldn't bring myself to tell Sophie that Gus was kind of right, too. Because she could barely stay upright in them. And she needed to tumble! It was in the script!

I usually didn't have any problems being direct and saying what I thought. But I couldn't get the words out.

And our problems went way beyond Sophie's shoes.

Gus riffled through his script one more time as everyone else fell into place.

"Wait a minute. Why is this ending different?" He shook the papers at me. "Did you rewrite this?"

"Actually, I did," Harper said. She flashed a silver smile at him. "I thought it needed some more EMOTION."

"You're both wrong," I reminded them. "I edited both your versions. I remember because it was around three-fifteen this morning and the moon was—"

"Luke!" Harper snapped. "You're not the writer!"

"That's right," Gus said. Inside his helmet, with only his eyes visible, he blinked fast. "I am."

"I wrote a bunch, too," Sophie said. "What happened to *my* edits?"

So this was what it felt like to have four people who all thought they were in charge of the script.

"We should go back to my original version," Gus insisted.

Sophie and Harper began arguing. I felt the frustration travel up my spine and down my arms, and I couldn't take the pressure anymore.

"We can't!" I burst out. "We're running out of time! None of this is going to work!"

The room quieted. After a few seconds, Harper reached out and patted my shoulder. "It's okay, Luke. Breathe."

I closed my eyes, took a deep breath in, and exhaled slowly, counting to ten. When I opened them, everyone was looking at me. (I think. It was hard to tell, since I couldn't quite track Gus's eyes.)

Harper replaced her mask and said, "Good job, bro. We're ready. Let's just try this version first."

"Thanks," I said, my voice a little shaky. I situated my phone, rejiggered the cord, and sent a wish into the universe that whatever trick Sophie had found to fix my phone connection was still working.

"Yesss!" I hissed. When I looked at the monitor, Harper, Gus, and Sophie all appeared to be floating in space, bright stars twinkling around them as a vast, deep darkness surrounded their on-screen bodies. It looked a little amateur hour, but it would have to do.

We set up our scene—me and Gus versus Sophie and Harper—and Sophie called, "Action!"

The Lorgans came at us with a slithering alien dance Harper had choreographed. Next to me, Gus was fighting back laughter as our sisters danced our way. But me? I was dead serious. In the zone.

As they advanced on us, Gus fake-fell backward in slow motion. "Nooooooo!"

Harper pounced. In the game, Lorgans killed humans by—fair

warning, this is pretty gross—scooping out their eyeballs, which they used to power their plasma cartridges. So Harper leaned over him, her fingers wiggling.

"I . . . want . . . your . . . eyeballs!" she moaned. I had bookmarked some realistic props I'd found on the internet the other day, including a set of very realistic fake body parts, but they cost money I didn't have. So for now, we were using grapes that we'd drawn on to give us that eyeball look. (Pun intended.)

"Cut," Sophie said immediately.

"What? Why? That was HIGH ART!" Harper complained.

"That's not your line!"

From the floor, Gus sighed. "I know I wrote it, but surely there's room for improv."

Sophie ripped off her mask and huffed.

We didn't have time for a sibling battle.

"Soph. Gus. Harper," I said. "Tick, tock."

"Fine," Sophie said. "I won't yell 'Cut!' anymore."

Phew. Crisis averted. Now we could get back to —

"Yoo-hoo!"

A sudden, urgent knock pounded at the basement door. With the way the Magees' house was set up, the basement door led right to the backyard.

"Argh!" Harper yelped. She ripped off her mask. What if whoever it was tried to break in? Our cover would be blown!

"Cut!" Sophie screamed.

"You already said that," Gus muttered.

"Hel-looooo!" came the voice at the door. With more pounding. Panic flashed across Sophie's face. *"It's Olivia!"* she mouthed.

Squeeeak went the doorknob. Yes, Olivia felt free to let herself in. Rowan Road was like that.

Gus leaped to his feet, sprinted across the room, and tore off his spheroidal dome helmet. He collided with the door just as it started to open. Then his shoulder slammed into the edge and he groaned.

Yeah, that was definitely going to leave a mark.

Which got me thinking about bruises as a concept. They're actually pretty cool. Back when I was little, I checked out any library book I could find that explained them and I watched a bunch of videos showing how blood from the affected capillaries leaks out and creates the purple and blue colors on the skin. I got the biggest bruise of my life when—

My train of thought (don't get me started on trains, I'll go for days) was interrupted by Olivia, still trying to get into the Magees' house.

"It's just little old me! Olivia!"

Gus's whole body braced against the door. His eyes were wild and bright. "Help?" he whispered.

Stepping forward, posture straight, Harper cleared her throat. In an accent I could neither place nor accurately describe, she called, "Can ve haaalllp youuuuu?"

I gaped at her. Gus blinked. Sophie threw a hand over her mouth.

"Al-lo? But who ees there?" Harper continued.

Sophie's shoulders started shaking.

Oh. Oh! Sophie was laughing! That kind of silent laugh, where something's so funny your body can no longer produce sound.

The kind of laugh that is more contagious than yawning.

I felt it coming up my throat. Oh no. I clasped both hands over my mouth.

Olivia knocked at the door again, but it sounded less confident. "O-live-ee-*a*. From up the street. Ms. Magee, is that you? I rang the bell but no one answered!"

Harper's brow furrowed. "O-live, you say? But ve do not know an O-live."

Tears ran down Sophie's cheeks. Gus looked bewildered, still barricading the door. My shoulders trembled.

"Um," Olivia said. "To whom am I speaking?"

"My dah-link, eet ees rude to knock on a door and demand to know who ees on ze other zide, ees eet not?" Harper countered.

Well, that did Sophie in. She fell to the floor, still silencing her laugh behind her hands.

Now Olivia sounded angry if a bit muffled by the door. "I'm just looking for the kids who live here! I need to talk to them. I have an idea about the block party!"

Who knew my sister really was a good actress?

"Vell, zey are not here. Go on and be done vith zis, please and thank you."

We all waited in silence. But Olivia didn't say anything else.

"The cameras!" I grabbed my phone and swiped to my app to

patch into the live feed of the Magees' backyard camera. Sure enough, there was Olivia, stomping away from the house.

Harper shook her shoulders and her head as if she was shaking off her character's persona. "Success!"

"Omigod," Sophie wheezed. "That was amazing."

Gus rubbed his shoulder. "Good job, everyone. Way to think fast, Harp."

She shrugged modestly. "It was no big thing."

We all made our way to the couch, which was pushed into the corner, and collapsed into our usual spots.

"That was way too close a call, though," Sophie warned.

Gus scratched his forehead, which made his hair stand up even taller than usual. "Agreed. Maybe we need to add Olivia to our PTS. I can't shake this feeling that she knows something."

I shook my head. "But the *P* stands for *parents*. We can't just add some random wannabe babysitter!"

"It doesn't need to be so literal, Luke," Harper reminded me.

"The point of the PTS is to track the whereabouts of people who might catch us and ruin everything!" Sophie pointed out. "And I hate to say it, but Gus is right. Olivia seems sus."

"Totally sushi," Harper agreed.

Gus raised an eyebrow. "Did you say 'sushi'? I'm starving."

"Fishy," Harper huffed. "Get it? Sushi? Fishy? Suspicious?"

I hated when things didn't fit like they were supposed to. But I knew she was right. Olivia needed to be tracked. Two close calls were two too many.

To, too, two, my brain repeated.

"Fine," I conceded. "But now, seriously? We have to get this done. According to the current PTS we won't have another free time to film until next week."

"And that is way too long to leave our fans hanging!" Harper cried. She flung her arms up passionately. "The algorithm will punish us!"

"Okay, okay," Sophie said. "Places, everyone!"

We all got up and made our way back to where we were. I repositioned the phone. I could easily splice these two edits together for a final version, if we could just get through this part . . .

"Action!"

Dashing to my spot off camera, I waited for my prompt. Harper managed to kill Gus, and even more impressive, she managed to stick to the script. Which meant Sophie was able to attack me just like we planned.

But just as Gus said the magic words to me ("Protect your eyes, brother!")—my signal to kick the Lorgans' laser blasters out of their hands and save us both—Sophie stumbled.

No. That wasn't the right word.

Accuracy was *important*.

As my brain tried to figure out what was happening, it was almost like Sophie was moving in slow motion.

In her shiny unitard, she stepped backward with her right leg to protect herself from my (fake) kick. But her boots were so high, and her legs so unsteady, that her ankle turned.

And I guess she was trying to catch herself, so she lunged to the side and swung her left leg around to catch her weight.

But her left foot was also in a sky-high boot. And when she tried to catch herself, her other ankle collapsed, too. And in an instant, those platform boots took Sophie down.

Safe to say . . . Sophie fell.

No, she wiped out. Like, *spectacularly*.

On camera.

Something inside my chest squeezed. Was she okay? Should I do something?

But Sophie was fine. She jumped right back to her feet, her mouth set in a straight line, and tried to get back into character. Nothing was broken . . . besides her ego.

Relieved, I panned the camera back to Harper and Gus, thinking maybe I could salvage this shot somehow. But Harper and Gus couldn't help themselves. They fell over, laughing, collapsing on the floor in front of Sophie, until all I could see through the camera lens was a messy pile of Lorgan and astronaut limbs.

"Cut," I sighed.

It wasn't until later that night, looking at the footage, that I realized just how perfect and funny Sophie's accidental fall was. (Maybe not in real life, but definitely on screen.) Inspired, and after a lot of jelly beans, I spliced our scenes together and added effects and music. I was about to send the file to Harper for posting when Sophie's face flashed before my eyes. I paused.

What if she was embarrassed?

I wouldn't be, but Sophie was different. She liked to be liked.

It was late. But I grabbed my phone anyway.

> [11:15 pm] Luke: How's your ankle
>
> [11:18 pm] Luke: Also I have to ask you something
>
> [11:29 pm] Luke: I guess you're asleep

My finger hovered over the file.

Harper was expecting the edited video . . .

And our fans were expecting a new post . . .

And Gus wanted to win the bet . . .

It was fine to post, right? Sophie knew her fall was caught on film. And she didn't say not to post it. So we were good.

Right?

I checked my phone again. Then my eyes roamed to my bed, which looked ready for me to drop into it.

My eyes grew heavy. The power of the jelly beans was wearing off.

Click.

★★★

User9905: DEAD DEAD DEAD this is the funniest thing I've ever seen [411,133 Likes]

yourmomjokesarefunny: Omg that girl wiped [13,559 Likes]

hannahbobannnn19: Crying, sobbing (did someone check on her, is she ok) [101,998 Likes]

thirdandmaple: Chat, I think she doesn't know how to walk in those shoes [6,541 Likes]

MaddielovesJoe: Give these kids their own YouTube series pls [287,008 Likes]

beckhamfan1433: Idk if this was planned or not but it's chef's kiss flawless [99,227 Likes]

hydrangela_baby: Skill issue [86,753 Likes]

123winning456: I NEED MORE OF THESE VIDEOS THESE KIDS ARE HILARIOUS [516,777 Likes]

Cre8saleslead: Those shoes are on sale right now, click here to purchase at a discount! [1,008 Likes]

OliviatheQueena: Seems staged to me, anyone else [655 Likes]

★★★

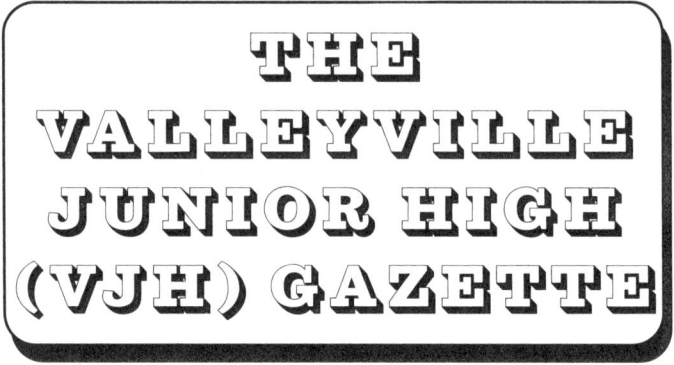

The latest news from grades 6–8

What's in: *Beauty and the Beast Jr.* auditions! Cast lists will be posted soon.

What's out: The first toilet stall in the second-floor girls' bathroom. Don't use it!

What's next: The boys' soccer team and girls' softball teams are both hosting home games this week. Show your spirit!

What VJH kids can't get enough of: *After Launch*! Read on for one sixth grader's take on the latest trend.

Students Rave about Viral Videos on Cre8

In our school-wide survey this winter, Valleyville Tigers voted Cre8 as "Favorite Place to Go for a Laugh." And now, students can't get enough of the hottest viral video on Cre8 these days: the *After Launch* parodies created by a mysterious group known as "HumansVsLorgans." This journalist can confirm: These videos are hilarious!

The videos star four friends posing as Lorgans, the terrifying (and kind of silly) alien creatures from the massively popular video game, and their enemy astronauts, who are trying to escape from Lorgan control so they can return home to Planet Earth. There are only two videos so far, but both are hilarious and unlike anything we've seen on Cre8. I'm not a big gamer myself, but even I know that *After Launch* is the top-selling video game in the country right now, and a feature film is currently in development. (I've been using my own Cre8 account to practice my audition techniques, so who knows? Maybe I'll star in the film!)

Valleyville seventh grader Jazzy G. said, "Everyone is obsessed with those videos. Even me, and I don't play video games!"

And eighth grader Sadie McSweeney said, "They ate. They absolutely ate and left no crumbs. We need more!"

If only we could find the mysterious team behind "HumansVsLorgans" . . . then we could start a social media campaign to get them to post even faster! But so far they have no other social media presence.

See you next week, VJH! Go, Tigers!

Selvi Gill, Grade 6

CHAPTER NINE
Sophie

I stomped so hard down the junior high hallway, roaring like an animal, that people actually moved out of my way.

"Harper June Gage-Flashman!" I shouted.

Fourth period had just ended, and technically I should have been headed to the cafeteria for lunch. But who could think about vegan nuggets and canned peaches at a time like this?

(Even though I actually loved those little peach cups.)

"Coming through!" I yelled as I pushed through the crowd. Backpacks were flying into my shoulders; someone's headphone cord looped around my wrist and jolted me backward; the warning bell pulsed in my eardrums. And still, all I could see was my target.

I cupped my hands around my mouth and called for her. *"Harp-er!"*

At the sound of her name, Harper whipped her head around. When she spotted me, fear flashed in her eyes for a second, but then her expression settled into an excited grin. Despite my palpable anger, she waved.

Well, that made me even more mad. Because who smiles and waves at a lion hunting for prey?

I'll tell you who: someone who thinks she's untouchable.

Someone who is used to me being easygoing and quick to please.

Someone who assumes I'll quit being angry, just like I quit everything else.

Well. I would show her!

I pushed through the final group of hungry kids until, finally, she was right in front of me.

"How. Could. You," I growled.

A hush fell over the crowd.

For a second, Harper's smile wobbled. But wow, she was a good actress, because before anyone else noticed, she transformed her face again. Now she was all happy and carefree. "Hi, Sophie," she said.

Now that I had her attention, I didn't quite know what to do with it. I had so much to say, but I couldn't even speak. I was angry, yeah.

But I was much more than that.

Aria, one of Harper's best friends, crinkled her nose. "Um . . . is everything okay here?"

Harper nodded once and side-hugged her friends. "Y'all, it's okay. Sophie and I just need to chat for a sec. It's a . . . neighborhood thing. We have some issues to work out. The block party . . ."

"Rowan Road gets weirdly serious about block parties," Lila reminded Aria.

Aria perked up a bit. "Think we'll score an invite?"

As her friends left, the rest of the crowd thinned out, too, moving toward the lunch line. Harper pulled me into the little alcove where the water bottle refill station emitted a constant whir.

"Listen," she began.

"No, *you* listen!" I hissed. "Harp, please take it down!"

She opened her mouth to respond but then closed it. Then she opened it again. Then she closed it.

"You look like a fish," I mumbled. My throat swelled up and my face got heavy. Especially behind my eyes.

Oh no. Was I about to *cry*? The last thing I wanted was more attention. That's what the whole problem was!

"It's gonna be okay," Harper started. "People are LOVING this one. You're a total star!"

"A star?" I repeated. I glanced down at my ankles, which looked so innocent. That morning, I'd buried those platform boots in my closet, never to be worn again. "Harper . . . that video is so embarrassing." To state what should have been obvious!

Harper nodded her head slowly, like she understood what I was saying but disagreed. "I promise, it's not. We would never try to embarrass you. We adore you!"

I shook my head, but Harper kept going. "Luke tried to text you last night. He was having second thoughts. But when we watched the edited version, we both nearly died laughing. It's the funniest blooper I've ever seen in my life! The world needed to see!"

My cheeks burned. Even my ears got hot.

"You've brought so much joy to the Cre8 community," she continued. "And see? People are obsessed with it. With you! We've already topped our first video!"

She proudly pulled out her phone and opened the app, showing me the rising numbers.

So Harper and Gus had won the bet—the one that I'd stupidly suggested. And by winning it, they'd made me a double loser. Lucky me.

"Soph." Harper grabbed my shoulders like she was about to pull me into a hug, but instead held me at arm's length. She looked so serious. "If there's one thing my acting lessons have taught me, it's that stepping outside of your comfort zone is the only way to grow."

I stared forlornly at the floor. Its big white tiles were always gleaming in the mornings, thanks to the janitorial staff. But now? They were scuffed and gray. They looked like kids had been stomping all over them all day.

Kind of like how I felt.

"Yeah, I don't need to grow like that," I insisted.

Harper squeezed my shoulders. "I'm gonna tell you a secret, Sophie Magee. Ready?"

I shrugged.

"You're the glue holding us all together," Harper said. "You're keeping the Rowan Roadies alive! This is your time to SHINE!"

Oh no. I sniffed. My eyes got watery.

If I cried now, I'd really lose it.

Did Harper really mean that?

"I know you think you're nobody special," Harper said.

"I don't know if I'd put it like that, exactly," I said.

"What I mean is, you're actually EXTRA special, and it's time you see that." She tossed her hair over her shoulder. It smelled like a summer day. "As creative director, I'm going to make it my mission for you to let the world see the REAL YOU. Through your Lorgan character, that is."

"You're not a creative director!" I reminded her, sniffling again. "You're a sixth grader who wants to be famous!"

She shrugged. "Same thing."

Harper couldn't imagine not wanting to be recognized. To be *seen*. And she really believed that everyone else wanted the exact same thing.

"Look," she continued gently. "If I thought it would make a difference now, I'd delete it. But there's no putting the toothpaste back in the tube. This thing has a life of its own."

Okay, I knew how the internet worked. Even if we deleted it from our Cre8 account, it had already been remixed and saved by tons of other accounts.

I don't know if it was Harper's words, or the truth that there was no going back. Or maybe it was just that canned peaches awaited me in the cafeteria. But some of my anger started to fade. And some of Harper's words began to sink in.

She wanted people to see the real me . . . through my Lorgan character.

Character.

I'd forgotten that I was playing a part.

I wasn't a total laughingstock on Cre8. *My character* was. Not *me*.

"Harper?" I asked suddenly. My tears had dried and my throat had sunk back to its normal size. "Why do you like acting so much?"

"Ooh!" Her eyes lit up. "I am SO happy you asked! It's positively an out-of-body experience to stand on a stage and pretend to be someone else. To INHABIT a different world. To EMPATHIZE with someone else's experience, just for a minute."

She got that dreamy look on her face, like she was picturing herself on the big screen.

I said, "So, you feel like that in a video shoot, too?"

"Oh sure," she sighed. "Acting is a chance to be someone else."

I blinked a few times, processing this information. Could I just have *fun* being an anonymous internet celebrity instead of getting all worked up?

Could I try to see what happened when I jumped into something headfirst? No more quitting, and no looking back?

My phone buzzed. We weren't technically supposed to have our devices on in class, but during lunch, kids usually caught up with their notifications.

It was a text from Luke.

Harper caught a glimpse of his name on my screen. "Oh, yeah, he told me he was going to check in on you. What's he saying?"

"'Sophie, I'm sorry for editing that video without asking you first. I won't do it again. Are you okay?'" I read aloud.

Hmm. That was . . . very nice of Luke, actually. To send an apology to me, and only me.

We had never texted each other before, privately. We'd only texted in the Rowan Roadie group thread.

"He's a good egg," Harper pointed out. Which was unnecessary, because I already knew who Luke was, at his core. I remembered that Luke knew me, too. Even when I didn't quite know myself.

"Earth to Sophie. Are you ever gonna tell me what's wrong?"

Across the lunch table, my best friend studied me. Jasmine "Jazzy" Wattana was tall, strong, passionate, and smart. She was the starting center on the Valleyville basketball team, one of the most talented artists in our grade, and could identify any song by the first opening note.

She was practically an icon. And I *hated* keeping secrets from her.

"Well, they ran out of peaches, for one thing," I huffed.

Just then, a dinner roll flew past my head, followed by some eighth grader crashing into our table as he caught a rogue football. Near the windows, a group of theater kids were belting out songs from *Matilda the Musical*, and over by the salad bar, some cheerleaders were practicing a stunt. Just another standard day in the cafeteria.

Except, when I looked closer, I could see groups of kids with their heads bent over phones. I could overhear snippets of our latest video. And over and over, the sound of me—Lorgan me—tripping and falling.

Our videos were *everywhere*!

"Here. This will make you feel better." Jazzy pushed her lunch tray toward me. She hadn't even opened her peaches yet!

Besties, man. They're . . . the best.

Still, I couldn't figure out a way to clue Jazzy into my situation without blowing our secret. Like, imagine saying, *Hey guess* what, I'm the star of two accidentally viral Cre8 videos! Want to sleep over tonight?

It simply wasn't possible.

"If you're not going to talk, can I tell you about this idea I had?" Jazzy said. Her eyes lit up.

I nodded, and she pulled out her phone. She tapped and swiped a few times, then flipped it to face me.

I froze, mid-peach-slurp.

Because Jazzy had opened Cre8.

"Check this out!" she said. "Cre8's hosting their first-ever talent contest!" She leaned over to tap a few more times while keeping the phone pointed at me. A new post from the admin team loudly advertised something called the *Cre8 and Captiv8 Contest*.

Jazzy said, "Remember how I told you my aunt taught me macramé? My sister, Malia, and I have been working on this big macramé project together, and we've been filming our progress—I don't even know why, just because. But now? We could turn our work into a submission and win a ton of money!"

I skimmed the contest announcement. The contest rules were straightforward: Any valid Cre8 account could submit one video, under three minutes in length and tagged with the #cre8contest hashtag, to "best capture the spirit of the Cre8 community." A team of celebrity judges would select twenty finalists, and then some mathematical mix of Likes and Comments from Cre8 users—along with input from the judges—would decide the winners.

And get this: The grand prize was a pot of money.

Like, a lot.

Was it weird that I immediately thought of Luke?

While we were filming the other night, Luke had made a few comments about how we needed better equipment and props. More realistic costumes that weren't fashioned from hand-me-downs and Halloweens past. More green screens, so we could film in larger spaces. Fancy special-effects software. That kind of stuff.

An image flashed before me. In it, I got to tell Luke that he could upgrade everything. That there was no budget to stick to. I pictured the grin on his face.

Not to mention . . . we'd probably have leftover money that we could use for other things, too. Like throwing the biggest block party this town has ever seen, so we could stop being known for ruining last year's!

It's like Harper had said . . . there was real money on the table with Cre8. And we were already famous, right? Might as well make it work for us.

"What do you think?" Jazzy asked. She blinked at me, waiting.

The dollar signs behind my eyes were big and flashy. But I guess I was too busy thinking about our videos to think about Jazzy's, and her face fell. "You hate the idea. Oh my gosh, you think I'm going to lose. You're right. Macramé is boring. No one wants to watch that! What was I thinking?"

"Jazz. Girl." I shoved the last peach into my mouth. "That's not it at all! You and Malia are so talented at macaroni!"

"Macramé." Jazzy's shoulders slumped.

"That's what I said," I replied, soothing her. "Seriously. You should do this! I just got distracted, that's all."

She eyed me curiously. "By what?"

Behind Jazzy, I spotted my brother getting back in line for a second lunch. "Gus!"

"What about him?" Jazzy looked baffled. Gus and I usually ignored each other in school.

I thought fast. "I need to check with him about something. That, er, block party our parents are planning. We have to do some damage control."

"You guys are so weird with these block parties," she muttered into her chocolate milk.

"Gotta run," I said. I grabbed my tray and backpack and made a start for Gus. Then I realized I was not being a very good bestie.

"Hey!" I called back to Jazzy. "You and your sister are totally gonna kill it with that malarkey!"

"Macramé!" Jazzy moaned.

"Gesundheit," I said, waving goodbye.

★★★

I grabbed my brother as he paid for his second lunch and steered him to an empty corner of the cafeteria for a smidge of privacy. As he wolfed down another helping of vegan nuggets, I filled him in on the Cre8 contest.

"So far, it looks pretty simple," I explained, showing him the announcement post. "They want to see 'creative, unique' submissions that 'reflect the vibe of your account.' And look—they say we should continue posting other content on our channel as usual."

"Got it," he said in between bites. Then he whistled at my screen. "There's a lot of fine print there."

I shrugged. "As Harper would say, details!"

"Ya know," he said, shoving the last nugget in his mouth and leaning back in his chair, "we could get better costumes with that prize money!"

"That's what I said!" I beamed. "I mean, to myself, in my head!" Obviously not to Jazzy.

Gus paused to take a long chug of apple juice. "Plus," he said, "new film equipment, a whole new set, more props, quality stage makeup . . . oh, and there's also this scriptwriting program I found. I'd love to buy that!"

"It's a no-brainer," I agreed.

Just this morning I'd been seething at our Cre8 content, and now here I was, trying to convince the Rowan Roadies to enter the contest! Life comes at you fast.

"Quick question, though," Gus said. "You seemed pretty mad this morning. You good?"

I didn't feel like getting all emotional again, so I kept it simple. "I had a long talk with Harper before lunch. And a text from Luke. They helped me see this whole thing from a new perspective."

Gus balled up his napkin and threw it on his tray. Then he shot me a huge grin. "So we're all in on this now?"

"All in," I said. I mean, we had a purpose now. An influx of cash! And so I got to work. Beginning with a text.

[12:10 pm] Sophie: Attention, Rowan Roadies: You're gonna want to check this out ➲ cre8.com/contest

[12:11 pm] Harper: !!!!!!!!!!!!!!!

[12:12 pm] Luke: Wow. That's a big prize . . .

[12:12 pm] Gus: And we'll reinvest every penny of it

[12:12 pm] Harper: I TOLD Y'ALL THIS WAS GONNA BE FUN!

[12:13 pm] Luke: PTS indicates that all parental figures and neighborhood pests are otherwise engaged today at three pm

[12:13 pm] Gus: So . . . that means 3 is open?

[12:13 pm] Luke: Confirmed

[12:13 pm] Gus: I just have to leave for a soccer game at 5

[12:14 pm] Harper: Ahhhhh I have so many ideas! How do we all feel about MUSICALS?

[12:14 pm] Gus: I'm not singing, Harper

[12:15 pm] Sophie: Actually . . .

We didn't *quite* get Gus to sing.

But later that day, in our basement, we quickly sketched out two videos that were pretty clever, if I do say so myself. Gus wrote one of them, and Harper and I tag-teamed on the other. Neither was for the contest—we'd need to really brainstorm on what our submission would be—but since Cre8 had said we should continue with our usual posting schedule, that's what we were doing.

"Since the contest counts both the judges' opinions *and* user engagement, keeping up our numbers is really important," Harper explained as we set up the shots. "The algorithm will be happy if we release more videos this week."

"I gotta be honest," Gus said. "I don't really know what an algorithm is."

Luke cleared his throat eagerly. "I can explain. At its simplest, an algorithm is a set of instructions. The more you interact with Cre8, for example, the better it gets at figuring out what you like, based on what you comment on, what you block, what you swipe past, and more."

"Gus, you probably get served a ton of soccer videos, right?" I said.

"Yeah," Gus said a bit glumly.

"While Luke gets shown people taking apart their computers," Harper added.

"Then there's me." I forced a laugh. "My algorithm is pure chaos."

"It's a fun experiment," Luke offered. He finished setting up his phone for filming and then studied me through the screen. "Next time you come across a video that's kind of different from what you usually watch, you should heart it. Soon you'll get more videos that are similar to *that* one."

"And that's how you tweak your algorithm," Harper said, smiling. Her face sparkled in her silver makeup. "Since our videos are doing well, we need to make more, and fast. That way, people who engage with us get served more from us!"

"So . . . the more successful your videos are, the more you should make?" I said.

Harper clapped her hands. "Exactly!"

"And for the contest, we'll have to create our best video ever, but it still has to match the rest of our content. Right?" I confirmed.

"Yep. We'll need to strategize, choose something that can take us to the next level. But for now, we have to keep posting regular content," Luke said.

"Feed the beast," Gus sighed.

"Welcome to the wonderful world of content creation," Harper said.

Luke tapped his screen. "Gus, we're ready. And . . . Action!"

The concept for this video had been Harper's idea, and I had to admit it was a great one. Cre8 was a go-to place for "get ready with me" videos, where people took viewers through their morning routine, with time stamps and a voiceover narration. We were calling this one "Get ready with me to defend our spaceship from the Lorgans" and Gus was the only one on-screen, so it was a breeze to shoot. He pretended to be getting dressed, stepping into his vac-suit and prepping for the battle, cracking *After Launch* jokes, and pretending to eat thermostabilized food, the kind that would be on board a spaceship. Obviously, he couldn't show his face, so we used some camera tricks to keep him anonymous. We wrapped it up in just twenty minutes!

When I yelled, "Cut!" Gus took off his helmet. His cheeks were pink. "Dude. It gets so hot in there."

"I'll see if I can rig some ventilation for next time," Luke offered.

"When we win the contest, we'll get breathable helmets," I confirmed.

"That was pretty good," Harper marveled. "Okay, my turn!"

To complement Gus's video, Harper was going to star in a "day-in-my-life" video. This involved narrating every step of a Lorgan's average day, starting with waking up and eating breakfast (in the video game, Lorgans didn't really eat anything, so we got creative with the names of fruits and vegetables), working out, and even painting a landscape of outer space to stay centered before attacking the human ships. In her unitard, silver and sparkly, Harper really did light up on camera.

I called, "Action!" and Luke decided to try out some closeups and zooms and other fancy camerawork for this one. It looked really good!

But when Harper reviewed the footage, she had some notes. "Let's do that part again, but we need some Lorgans in the background for ambiance," she said.

"Ambiance?" Gus mouthed to me.

Harper continued. "Sophie, suit up. And Gus? Put some of that silver makeup on. Just, like, dust it all over your face. Here's a beanie for your hair."

I quickly pulled on my Lorgan costume as Gus glanced at his watch. "I have, like, five minutes."

"You're just a background player for this one, no worries!" She plopped the gray beanie on his head and helped him smear silver lipstick from his forehead to his chin while I did the same.

"PTS advises we close the set in ten minutes," Luke noted.

"We're going as fast as we can!" Harper hurried, zipping a gray hoodie on Gus. She pointed out where we would stand and gave us some quick directions.

"Action!" Luke directed.

In the background, Gus and I acted like Lorgans getting ready for the day as Harper sat up close to the camera, describing a typical Lorgan breakfast and explaining how the kazooksa-berry-tot was native to the Lorgans' home planet. I was standing there, trying not to laugh, when my eyes landed on Gus's watch by accident.

"Cut!" I yelled.

CHAPTER TEN
Gus

I ran as fast as I could, the streets of Valleyville blurring past me like the scenery on a high-speed train. As I approached, I began to hear the cheers of the crowd and the shrieks of the referees' whistles. The game—my first of the season—was in full swing.

Maybe I was worrying for nothing, I thought, sprinting the final block. Maybe my parents were late, too. Maybe there'd been traffic, or a train delay. Or a work emergency. Or maybe they hadn't missed me yet?

Yeah, right.

That was one great thing about my parents. They were really good about showing up for us kids. At least one of them was always at the events that mattered: first games, playoff games, important try-outs, end-of-season awards ceremonies. They were always there for parent-teacher conferences, or to help us with our homework, or to drive us to a school dance. They were, basically, *awesome* at fulfilling their parental duties.

Too bad I wasn't so great at my kid duties. What kind of center forward doesn't show up on time to his first game of the season?

I didn't have time to beat myself up about it, though, because just then I saw them. They were standing at the gates to the field, and if

I squinted hard enough, I could practically see those cartoon tension lines radiating out of their heads. They were *stressed*.

"Mom! Dad!" I yelled, closing the distance between us. Their heads snapped up from their phones. (They'd probably been checking my location and sending texts to anyone I'd ever met.) When they caught sight of me, they came jogging over, relief all over their faces.

"Gus! You okay? We've been calling you!" Mom did that parent thing where she scanned my face and body, cupping my cheeks and ruffling my hair, to make sure I wasn't bleeding. Or worse.

"I didn't hear it," I said honestly. My phone was buried somewhere in my duffel bag, and I'd been running so fast, I never heard the ringtone.

Dad's eyebrows shot up. "You're fine, though? Not hurt or anything?"

Still trying to catch my breath, I nodded. Other than being sweaty, exhausted, and worried about Coach, I was fine! "I'm really sorry. I got caught up doing . . . um, this school project."

They both looked skeptical. I flashed back to what we'd told Tara the morning after our first video went viral. It was important to keep our stories straight if we wanted to stay under the radar. "On how Taylor Swift's songwriting uses a lot of historical references. Like, about World War One and dinosaurs and stuff."

"Gus." Mom held my face and looked into my eyes. "We'll talk after the game. For now, though?"

She paused, and my stomach dropped. Was she going to ground me? Pull me from the team? Send me to my room?

Instead, she grinned. "Get out there and kick some butt!"

★★★

When Coach saw me jog up to the sideline, he did a double take, tucked his baseball cap more firmly over his head, and turned away. Yeah, he was mad. I dumped my bag onto the ground and slunk onto the bench.

Out on the field, Colton blocked an attempt and I clapped, trying to get my head into the game. This was fine. Everything was fine! Coach would get over it once I got out there and scored. Right?

But then Austen sidled up to me on the bench. He squirted his water bottle into his mouth and eyed me up and down.

"What?" I said, annoyed, my eyes flicking back and forth between him and the field. Ryan Ling tripped and took a tumble, which made the visiting team swoop in and steal the ball. Within seconds, they had reversed course and scored a perfect goal.

I groaned, along with the rest of the crowd. But Austen's eyes were still on me.

"What?" I repeated, more annoyed this time. "I know I was late."

"Uhhh . . ." Austen pointed at the area above my ear. "What is that?"

Swatting away what I assumed was a bug, I shrugged.

But Austen shook his head. "No . . . I don't think that's gonna do it." His eyes widened. "Wait a minute. I know. You got a job as a clown for kids' birthday parties?"

"Huh?" I muttered. But whatever. I wasn't going to let Austen get me in more trouble with Coach. If he saw us goofing around like this, he'd probably launch into outer space.

"Just admit it, dude," Austen said. "Maybe you can do a magic trick for us later."

"Clowns don't do magic tricks, genius. Magicians do," I muttered. Still sweaty from my run, I scratched the back of my neck, which was wet and gross.

And also . . . gray? I glanced at my fingers.

Not gray. *Silver.*

"Gimme," I growled at Austen, who had just taken his phone out of his bag and was trying to record me. I ripped it out of his hands and turned the camera to myself to use as a mirror.

I gasped.

I'd had a ton of Lorgan makeup on me, thanks to Harper. But while I was running, I'd rubbed this cold, slimy wipe-thing all over my face, which Harper had tossed to me before I'd bolted out the door. I'd thought I'd gotten all the makeup off, but of course there was no time to check.

Now there were silver swirls all over my ears, my neck, even stuck in my eyebrows!

I frantically wiped the makeup off while Austen cracked up. I was almost done when I heard the unmistakable sound of Coach's whistle.

"Magee! Get in there, now!"

Dashing past Coach and onto the field, I heard him say, "And what the heck is all over your face?"

★★★

We won the game, 3–1. I scored the final goal, which meant Coach would probably forgive me. To celebrate, my family headed to dinner at our favorite restaurant—Sophie and Luke had arrived at the game during halftime. Not a speck of silver makeup could be found on them, which felt very unfair.

Dad gave a play-by-play of the most exciting parts of the game, as though I hadn't been there myself and, you know, scored the very goal he was talking about. It made me wonder, and not for the first time, if he liked soccer even more than I did.

The restaurant sat us quickly, which was good luck because I was about to pass out from hunger. The server took our orders and, in addition to my deluxe chicken panini with fries and onion rings and extra bacon, I also ordered a bunch of appetizers for the table.

Just when I thought I was in the clear, Mom took a sip of her iced tea and said, "So. What happened, Gus?"

Sophie kicked me under the table. My eyes flicked back and forth between my parents. This felt like a trick question.

Luckily, the appetizers arrived, and we all took down some nachos and mozzarella sticks. Whoever invented appetizers deserves an award.

"I lost track of time," I reminded them, but to me it sounded weak. "It won't happen again." Especially the forgetting-to-remove-my-makeup part.

"If this school project is taking up too much of your time, we can talk to Coach," Mom offered.

"That's what he's there for, kid," Dad agreed. "Everyone, including your teachers, understands how important it is to balance soccer and school."

"That seems a bit unfair . . ." Sophie said under her breath.

I kind of agreed, but I kept my mouth shut. There was like this unspoken agreement with teachers to give me lots of flexibility with homework, just in case I got to be a pro player someday. One of my friends from travel team even had permission to skip his electives so he could get training time in the gym! That sounded like the worst of all worlds to me. I loved my electives—especially creative writing.

"Thanks, Mom, but I don't need help with the project," I said. I felt bad for lying, but I was in too deep now.

"The project is almost over anyway," Sophie piped up. She grabbed the last mozzarella stick and winked at me. "Right?"

"Wait a minute," Mom said. "You were with your brother?"

Sophie froze, the mozzarella stick hovering between the table and her mouth.

But Dad was delighted. "You two were hanging out together? On purpose?"

"That's great," said Mom. "I love when you two spend time together. But . . . can you keep a closer eye on the clock next time?"

"Totally," Sophie assured her. "All of us will."

"Oh, who else is in your project group?" Mom wondered.

"Just Harper and Luke," I said, leaning back as the server delivered a steaming panini. Heaven on a plate.

"Sophie and the Gage-Flashmans? Did y'all take a time machine back to elementary school?" Dad joked.

"Yeah, it's fun hanging out all together again," Sophie chirped. "And it makes it easier for you guys, right? Now you two can see more of Tara and Brynn!"

"Sounds good to me," Dad said. "As long as you remember to balance both soccer —"

"And school," I said dully.

"Bingo." He nodded.

"Let's talk about what that looks like *in practice*," Mom said. We'd been so close to putting this entire subject to bed . . . which by the way was very much where I wanted to go as soon as we got home . . .

"Mom," I said to her, "I know how to balance. It's all good."

She shrugged. "I'm just saying. Being late to your first game is so unlike you. So maybe you should take a break from all this socializing? I can tell Tara and Brynn that you're off-limits for a while."

What? No!

"Good thinking," Dad added, his mouth full. "Just until you adjust to your schedule. Or even until soccer season is over."

"But . . ." With all the leagues and camps I was in, soccer season was *never* over!

"Let's see what the calendar says . . ." Mom put down her fork and picked up her phone. "Okay, Coach has you in double sessions for the next four weekends, and you have two games a week . . . plus there's that optional information session coming up for the summer team, and there's this special lecture for kids interested in D-1 athletics . . ."

My brain shut down then. Like, it seriously short-circuited. I shoved the rest of the onion rings in my mouth and tried to breathe. Sophie mouthed, *"Sorry. We'll figure it out."*

But she was wrong. When Mom and Dad got going, they never stopped. Sure, they thought they were doing what was best for me. But hearing how my whole calendar was booked, how my whole life was already planned . . . when would I get to write? To film? To just be a kid?

And why did they need to butt in just when we needed to submit our best video to Cre8?

★★★

Harper and Luke kept texting about our contest submission, but I avoided them. I even avoided Sophie a little bit, just so I could think. Sometimes it seemed like I was only allowed to care about one thing, which wasn't fair, because everyone else seemed to be able to do whatever they wanted. On the other hand, maybe my parents had a point. I'd messed up today. Maybe two major things in my life was one too many?

I was about to sneak downstairs for a snack when my phone lit up again.

[7:33 pm] Harper: Earth to the Mageees 🌎

[7:35 pm] Harper: I know you're home. I can see both of you through your windows.

[7:36 pm] Luke: They make these things called curtains now, fyi

Through the bedroom wall, I heard Sophie snort.

[7:37 pm] Sophie: We're not avoiding you

[7:37 pm] Harper: Omg, you're TOTALLY avoiding us

[7:38 pm] Luke: You both need to fill out your section of the PTS

[7:38 pm] Harper: We HAVE to get started on our contest submission

[7:38 pm] Harper: Also our latest video is not doing as well as the others

[7:38 pm] Harper: Like, I'm wondering if Cre8 is down? Is it working for you guys?

[7:38 pm] Harper: It's just weird. The first two times we hit a million views by the 24-hour mark, but this one is nowhere near that . . . and the comments are NOT IT

[7:38 pm] Harper: Then again . . . it's definitely NOT our best video *cough cough no thanks to Gus leaving early cough cough*

[7:39 pm] Luke: Harper's had a lot of sugar today

[7:40 pm] Gus: Lucky

[7:40 pm] Harper: He speaks! HE'S ALIIIIIVE

[7:40 pm] Sophie: Barely

[7:41 pm] Harper: Uh oh. What happened? DRAMA!

[7:42 pm] Gus: Mom and Dad are worried that I'm getting too distracted

[7:42 pm] Gus: Honestly maybe they're right

[7:43 pm] Sophie: Excuse me what?

[7:43 pm] Sophie: For the first time I decide NOT to quit something, and you're quitting instead?

[7:44 pm] Harper: That's some Freaky Friday kinda stuff!

[7:44 pm] Gus: Not quitting. Just . . . thinking. Wondering. Look at the numbers. What if we're not as good as we thought we were? What's the point of spending all this time on Cre8? I was late to my game and for what?

[7:45 pm] Harper: I don't get what you're saying

[7:46 pm] Gus: Like . . . we're spending all this time to make awesome videos but not getting any credit for it. We're anonymous!

[7:47 pm] Harper: Wait a minute. You left early for the game, which meant we couldn't perfect the video, but you were late anyway? And then I had no choice but to post a video that was MID at best, and now it's flopping?

[7:48 pm] Sophie: That's kinda harsh, Harper.

[7:48 pm] Gus: Dude. Are you trying to blame me for low views? Aren't you the one who wrote it? Maybe people just don't like it!

[7:49 pm] Harper: Oh, because I'm not an expert writer like you? Now you're some kind of savant?

[7:49 pm] Gus: . . . I don't know even know what that means

[7:50 pm] Harper: I REST MY CASE!

[7:51 pm] Gus: You know what? I don't need this stress. I'm under enough pressure already. Bye.

That did it. I did something no kid ever does willingly: I turned off my phone. Did the world's best soccer players waste their time on social media? Were award-winning novelists spending hours sending texts? No and no.

I needed a break from my friends and a break from Cre8.

TheHarbourTriplets: This was kinda funny but nothing like the other ones [23,112 Likes]

StarGirl_1989: The last thing Cre8 needs is more GRWM videos, boo [14,190 Likes]

Yo_itsSmitty: Gonna go watch the earlier videos and pretend this one never happened [11,766 Likes]

user_345987: How did I end up on this. The algorithm is failing me [8,432 Likes]

Socratease: Give us more bloopers! [7,998 Likes]

MaddiewuzHere: Thank u, next [7,132 Likes]

Rail_fan_99: NOT thank u, next [6,559 Likes]

OliviatheQueena: Told y'all. These videos are nothing special [244 Likes]

CHAPTER ELEVEN
Harper

The first rule of fashion: When you're in a foul mood, put on your favorite outfit.

Head held high, my hair long and shiny, my lips pink and glossy, I waltzed through the halls of Valleyville Junior High in a rainbow-striped blouse and a pair of sparkly green pants. *Swish-swish*, they said with every step, announcing my arrival. *Here comes Harper June Gage-Flashman!*

It was a big day. Today, Ms. Hopper was posting the cast list for the spring musical. And as I mentally prepared for the role of a lifetime that was coming my way, I decided to steer clear of the Rowan Roadies for the day. Let them argue amongst themselves about Cre8. I had REAL DRAMA to focus on.

Now, listen. I'm an OPTIMIST. And even though my audition didn't start out great, I was confident my reputation, and my general PIZZAZZ, would grant me some grace.

In other words, I knew Ms. Hopper and Mr. O wouldn't hold my root beer burp against me. In fact, it was probably a plus in my column. It proved how well I can project my voice!

Right?

Despite my confidence, though, I woke up so far on the wrong side of the bed that I was actually UNDER it. (Literally. What can I say? I sleepwalk. In fact, I was forbidden from sleeping over at Lila's house after her mom found me passed out on the floor of her closet one morning.)

I wasn't used to failure. It tasted BITTER and TOO SALTY. So, this Cre8 flop had me really scratching my head. It hadn't been long since we'd become famous, but now I was used to it!

I didn't like the feeling of fighting with Sophie and Gus. I knew I hadn't been MY BEST SELF. But I didn't think I deserved ALL the blame for our video flopping!

And maybe . . . just maybe . . . I also felt like I had something to prove.

Because if I, Harper June Gage-Flashman, couldn't become a star on Cre8, how would I become one in real life?

All of this was swimming through my head as I tugged open my locker and dumped my math book inside. It landed with a satisfying *thump*.

"Hey, girlie! Today's the big day!"

I spun around to find Aria and Lila. We had OF COURSE coordinated our outfits that morning, so Aria was in her rainbow polka-dot romper, and Lila was in a plain white sweater and jeans with little rainbows embroidered all over them.

I appreciated that my best friends had let me be the only one of us who sparkled today. After all, what were friends for?

We squealed and hugged and jumped up and down like we did every morning when we first saw each other. Then I cleared my throat and smoothed my hair. "I am BEYOND excited!"

"What time does the cast list get posted again?" Lila asked.

"When the fourth period bell rings," I reminded her. Ms. Hopper did things old-school. She taped an actual piece of paper on the door to the auditorium at lunchtime. So quaint! So CHARMING! This is why I loved theater people so much. We understand tradition! Anticipation! COMMUNITY!

"I can't believe our girlie is going to be the lead in the school musical!" Aria chirped, giving me a bonus hug.

"Well," I said, trying to blush. "We'll see."

It was important to stay modest, even on the edge of your big break.

All morning, it felt like people were looking at me. Like they knew I was on the precipice of fame and they wanted to see it for themselves. If only they realized I was ALREADY FAMOUS. And that they'd been obsessed with me for weeks!

I mused on that some more while Señor Delgado was teaching us about present simple tense. What did it mean, I wondered, to be secretly famous? Did it feel the same as being regular, not-secretly famous? Sometimes, I wished I could tell everyone in school that it was ME they were watching on their phones. That it was ME who had taken over Cre8 and gotten everyone doing the "Lorgan dance." That it was ME who was about to win the inaugural Cre8 contest, which would catapult me into the upper echelon of influencers!

Well, US. The Rowan Roadies. Not just me, I had to remind myself.

The morning dragged on and on. But finally, it was time for lunch, which meant the cast list was about to be posted. When I passed Luke in the hall, he shot me a thumbs-up and a smile, which FORTIFIED me. He's a good brother, underneath it all.

I met up with Aria and Lila outside the Spanish room and we linked arms, giggling the whole way to the auditorium.

My heart was RACING. My hair was FLOATING. I was so ready to start my journey as the most captivating Belle the world had ever seen! (Minus Emma Watson, our queen.)

The three of us were so focused on beating the crowds in the hallway that I didn't watch where I was going.

"Oof!" I blurted when my shoulder hit someone's backpack. We had just rounded the final corner to the auditorium, which was crammed with kids. "Sorry!"

"Watch where you're going," a voice snapped

It was none other than Selvi Gill! I glared at her. My NEMESIS.

But then Selvi burst into laughter. "Just kidding, Harper. No big deal. It's so crowded here! Hey, are you as nervous as I am? This is so stressful!"

Sometimes I forgot that Selvi was . . . actually nice.

And not really my nemesis at all.

After all, it's not HEALTHY to have nemesises (nemeses? I made a mental note to look it up later!) in middle school. It's also not good for your skin, and as an actress, my skin was VERY IMPORTANT to me. I did a lot of facial masks and creams, even though my moms were always telling me to chill out with the skincare.

Selvi and I were always up for the same roles, not just at school but even in summer theater camps. It wasn't HER fault that she was the second-most-talented actress in our grade.

Maybe it was time for me and Selvi to join forces. Stardom would surely be easier if I had a friend who understood me, wouldn't it? That's how it was with the Rowan Roadies these days. Having people who GET you is priceless.

Especially when you're navigating things like fame . . . and middle school.

I shot Selvi my biggest, gleamiest smile.

"I am SO nervous," I assured her. And then, feeling generous, I linked arms with her, too, and we four girls pushed our way through all the other kids, craning our necks.

"I see it!" Aria shouted. "It's up!"

I was so jumpy, even my hair was sweating. This was it. A moment I would remember forever. When I won my first Oscar, I would stand onstage and tell THIS VERY STORY to remind my fans that even though I was the most famous actress the world had ever seen, I was still also a HUMAN BEING who had gone through HARD TIMES that made me VERY RELATABLE. And also HUMBLE. And that would make them all love me even more! And then I would—

"Oh no," Lila murmured.

I stopped my daydreaming and tried to focus.

"It's okay, babe," Aria chirped. "The ensemble is so important!"

"And we'll be doing it together, which makes it even more special!" Lila gave me one more hug.

Ensemble?

Did she say ENSEMBLE?

I might have been a B-student in Spanish, but even I knew what *ensemble*, from the French *ensemblée*, meant.

Being in the ensemble meant you didn't have a speaking role.

It meant you were a background singer.

Part of the chorus.

My chest felt funny. My arms slipped out from my friends' grips and I pushed through the group of kids until I was standing directly in front of the cast list.

My eyes had to be playing tricks on me. Because my name wasn't at the top of that list as I'd expected.

And it wasn't midway down, either.

It was at the bottom, where it said, clear as day, that I, Harper June Gage-Flashman, would be playing the role of . . . ENSEMBLE NUMBER ONE.

"I mean, number one! Isn't that great?" Lila laughed, and was it me, or did she sound nervous? "I'm number eight! You're so much higher than me!"

Aria—number six— nodded furiously. "You're the lead in the ensemble! It's a win!"

"The lead in the ensemble is almost better than being the actual lead," Selvi added. She smiled weakly. "Who wants to be in all those rehearsals anyway? Poor Caitlin!"

Caitlin Weber was in eighth grade and had been performing for years. I shouldn't have been surprised that she'd been selected as Belle, but . . . I was. How could anyone watch ME onstage and still pick someone else?

GASP! Selvi was named one of the three village girls who are obsessed with Gaston. That was an actual SPEAKING ROLE. A small one, but still. Dialogue!

Speaking of . . . well, speaking: I couldn't do it. My mouth simply would not let me.

Was this what it felt like to HYPERVENTILATE?

My breath was doing this funny thing where it couldn't calm down, and my hands were shaking. Shivering? I backed up, my vision spotty, bumping into people and backpacks and eventually the cold concrete wall of the hallway, until my legs collapsed under me and I was sitting on the floor, stunned.

All those monologues Selvi had posted to her Cre8 account . . . was it possible they had helped her?

Meanwhile, I'd been spending all my spare time hiding my real identity. Ms. Hopper had no way of knowing that I was way more famous than Selvi; that I'd expanded into writing and directing, too. Because I couldn't tell her! I couldn't tell ANYONE.

And if I couldn't tell anyone I was famous . . . what was the point?

★★★

There's only one thing to do when you're feeling this down.

"Mommy?" I whispered into my phone. I was in the bathroom

outside the school library, which was always the least-used bathroom, and the only place I could think of where there might be some privacy.

"Harp? What's wrong?" Mom B said.

"I think I'm sick," I said. For good measure, I forced a cough. It TOTALLY sounded real.

How could a girl who could cough *so* convincingly not get the lead in the school musical?! I bet Caitlin Weber's fake cough was ridiculous.

I had called Mom B over Mom T for a couple reasons. For one, Mom T was a whole train ride away in her office in the city while Mom B worked from home. And two, because Mom B was way more likely to tuck me into bed and make me chicken soup. She just has that way about her. So, in no time, I was picked up, whisked away, and tucked gently into my bed, Poodle purring happily on my shoulder.

Mom B poked at me a bit—METAPHORICALLY—to find out what was on my mind.

"I wish you'd tell me what's really wrong," she murmured after taking my temperature for the fourth time (it was perfect) and casually mentioning that I hadn't coughed a single time since she'd picked me up from school.

I sighed dramatically.

"What happened at school? Was it a bad grade? A—oh!" Mom B's face changed. She remembered—I could see it. "Oh, honey. Today was the big day, right? The cast list?"

I tried to pull my comforter up to hide my face, but she was sitting on it and I couldn't tug it free. Also, with a face like mine, it's just not FAIR to hide it away, even for a second.

So I bravely faced my truth. "I didn't get a part."

Her jaw dropped. "I thought everyone who auditioned would get a part."

I waved my hand away. "By that I mean, I just got the ensemble. Ensemble singer number one, to be exact."

Mom B exhaled, looking relieved. And, oddly, kind of proud. "Honey, that's wonderful. You're a beautiful singer! This will be such a fun experience for you!"

"But . . ." How could I explain without giving away my secret? "I really wanted a bigger part, Mom."

"Baby." She smiled at me. "So what if you aren't the star this time? You have to have something to reach for. To dream about. You'll get there if you keep working at it. I promise!"

I know she meant well. And for any other kid who hadn't gotten the lead, that would've been the perfect way to reassure them. But not me. Because I was ALREADY famous. And nobody was giving this star her due!

Then again . . .

I could feel a spiral coming. Because what if I—GASP!—wasn't as good an actress as I thought I was?

I had to face facts. My latest Cre8 video was a dud. I had barely eked out a part in the musical. Clearly, everyone hated me. The world thought I was a hack!

And to make matters worse . . . I could never have root beer again. Not after the way it had betrayed me during my audition, which was CLEARLY a major reason I didn't score a better part. Not even a root beer float! Root beer was DEAD TO ME!

"Oh, Poodle!" I buried my head in her soft white fur. "You're the only fan I have left!"

"That's not true," Mom B assured me, but I was too far gone, lost in the ways I had reached for the stars, only to end up in the gutter.

I was starry LITTER, when all along I'd thought I was starry GLITTER.

My hopes for making a name for myself in junior high were going up in smoke, right alongside my dreams of becoming a Cre8 influencer-turned-sitcom-star-turned-youngest-Marvel-superhero-ever.

I'd really thought Cre8 would get it all started. But it turned out, I'd been very wrong.

Poodle, thank goodness, knew I needed her now more than ever. She tucked herself into my neck, purring like a broken motor, while Mom B tried to convince me to keep going.

"This is just a minor setback," she soothed, flicking Poodle's tail out of my eyes. "You have so much potential. You just have to keep doing what you love!"

I flung my hands dramatically over my eyes. One of them whacked Poodle's backside and she leaped off me, offended. She darted out the door.

Even my cat was abandoning me!

CHAPTER TWELVE
Luke

I was starting to feel it again.

It.

How I used to feel when I was little, back before we had a name for it: dysregulated.

I still *felt* things harder than Harper did. As a kid, washing my hair physically hurt me, and needing to take a detour could throw off my whole day. Now, I knew how to work around things, mostly.

But now that everything was just *off*, my body and my brain were both feeling it. And it was making me jittery, like how Mom T says she gets when she has too much coffee.

To start with, Harper wasn't herself. I mean, she didn't even *look* like herself! After the cast list was posted, she'd started wearing all black clothing. No rainbows, no sunbursts, no inspirational sayings in sequins. But our moms and I didn't say a word. It felt too risky.

Meanwhile, Gus had basically ghosted all of us. He hadn't logged anything in the PTS all week, and every time I saw him in school, he was very busy chatting with a teacher or joking with his teammates. He said he needed a break, but I thought he meant from Cre8, not from *us.* And then there was Sophie. Just when she'd decided she *did* want to be a Cre8 star, our plans had completely fallen apart! I wondered how she was doing, but I wasn't sure how to ask.

While the Magees' trampoline sat empty, I started to wonder if this was how it felt to have whiplash. I'd been fine before the Rowan Roadies came back together. Seriously! Some kids might consider me a loner, but I had everything, and everyone, I needed. Still, I couldn't deny that it was nice to have a group to hang out with again. Sharing a secret with them had changed me a little bit. I'd gotten used to having them around again, and without them, I felt a little lost.

The vibe shifts at home and at school weren't helping. My moms were treading carefully around Harper, trying to convince her she still had a future in theater. Poodle crept around corners and hid under furniture. And at school, I couldn't figure out how to get back to normal! I had this wild secret, and if I told it, I could change everything.

But did everything *need* to change? Wasn't I just fine before?

When I was little, the Rowan Roadies had been a type of protection, almost. But that protection disappeared by the time we got to junior high. And I'd been okay with that. I didn't need anybody but me to get by. Until Cre8 came along and showed me that it wouldn't be such a bad thing if more people knew who I was.

I hadn't realized posting some videos would be so exhausting. So complicated.

And after a couple days of this mess, with no one really talking to each other and all the color gone from our lives, I just couldn't take it anymore.

I needed my body and my brain to start listening to each other again.

"Harp? What's with the clothes?"

We were all in the living room. It was that time of evening where it was too early to go to bed but too late to do anything else. Mom B was half watching something on TV while Mom T was browsing her laptop. I was on the recliner, biting my nails and trying to follow Mom B's show, but it was in French and had captions, and it didn't feel right to be reading the TV. You know what I mean? Things need to be *right*.

My sister was sitting on the stool at our kitchen island. And by sitting, I mean literally just sitting. Nothing else! She wasn't watching (or reading) TV. She wasn't on her phone; wasn't browsing one of those gossip websites she loved. She didn't even have Poodle to keep her company!

"I'm glad you asked," Harper said solemnly. She cleared her throat. "I have a family announcement."

But just at that moment, something happened on Mom B's show and she yelped. That made Mom T jump, and her laptop slid off her lap and onto the floor. And that made Poodle, who'd been hiding under the couch, run in fear. Her claws scratched against the wood floors and knocked into the leg of the coffee table, where Mom B's giant bowl of freshly popped popcorn wobbled until, finally, it tilted over and dumped its contents all over the floor.

"Oh no!" Mom T said.

"*Poodle!*" Mom B groaned.

"Ahem," Harper tried again.

I pointed to my sister. "Your cat, your mess."

"Enough." Mom T, hands on hips, shot us both a look. "Harper, get the vacuum, and then tell us your news."

Looking like a shadow in her all-black clothes, Harper quickly swept up the popcorn while our moms put the bowl in the kitchen and fixed the wobbly coffee table. When things were back to normal, Harper stood in front of the TV, facing us like she was going to put on a show.

Which would not be unusual!

"My news," she began, using some kind of accent I couldn't place, "is that I've made the decision to turn down the ensemble role I was offered in the musical. Instead, I'll be taking up competitive duck herding."

Mom B snorted. Mom T's jaw tightened.

I blinked. "You're going to listen to ducks?"

"Huh?" Harper's face crinkled, then she sighed, as if I was the one who'd said something silly. "*Herding.* Not heard-ing."

"Hurting?" I said. I was horrified. "You can't hurt animals, Harp! What is happening to you?!"

"Mo-oms!" Harper huffed.

"Luke, get a dictionary. Harper, absolutely not," Mom T said. She was clearly out of patience with both of us.

Harper's eyebrows shot up. Wait a minute. Was she wearing black eyeliner?

Mom T crossed her arms. "You made a commitment, Harper June. Just because you didn't get the role you wanted doesn't mean it's okay to quit."

Next to her, Mom B winced. In a low voice, she said to Mom T, "We talked about this. We said—"

"No." Mom T shook her head. "Harper needs to learn this lesson. We love you so much, sweetie, but you're not always going to be the star, and you have to learn that that's okay."

My eyes volleyed back and forth between my moms. They never disagreed! Their disagreement was making my skin itch all over again. And I still didn't understand what was going to happen to all the ducks!

"Very well." Harper stiffened her shoulders. Her eyes landed on mine. "But I will be stopping any and all other drama-based activities."

Both of my moms looked confused. "What other drama activities are you signed up for?" Mom B wondered.

But I knew.

Harper and I stared at each other. It was like she was trying to send me a message without letting our moms in on it.

Well, message received. Because I understood perfectly what Harper was saying. Or, was *not* saying. Or . . . whatever. This is why it's confusing when people don't say what they mean!

Harper wanted to quit the musical, but she wasn't allowed.

But our moms didn't know about our *After Launch* videos. So they couldn't stop her from quitting those.

Gus was out, and now Harper was out, too.

There would be no Cre8 contest submission. No more Cre8 videos at all! No fame; no fortune. I wouldn't be able to get that new camera equipment I'd already bookmarked on my laptop; or the expensive special effects software I'd started dreaming about.

But, when I really thought about it, I was losing a lot more.

There'd be no more group texts, no more jokes, no more hangouts on the trampoline or in the Magees' basement.

No more inside jokes, no more Lorgan dancing, no more feeling like I had a place in the world.

I'd go back to being alone. Just the way (I thought) I liked it.

Another weekend came and went. I spent most of it holed up in the basement playing anything I could find that wasn't *After Launch*.

Was it just me, or did every video game suddenly stink?

When Monday morning rolled around, Mom T took Harper to an orthodontist appointment, so I trudged to school alone. It was another perfect spring day; so warm that, before I'd even reached the end of our driveway, I shrugged off my hoodie and stuffed it in my already-overstuffed backpack. I put on my big headphones and an old episode of my favorite tech podcast and tried to zone out as I started down the block.

I was deep in my own world for the next little while, remembering how I was an expert at doing my own thing.

So obviously I was shocked when someone tapped my shoulder.

"Argh!" I jumped, ripping off my headphones.

"Sorry," Sophie said, stepping backward.

My heart raced. She had really surprised me!

In my defense, the mysterious new house that confused everyone in town had just come into sight. Or maybe it was just me? "You know I hate jump scares, Soph, especially while we're near The Black Hole!"

Her faced brightened at the memory. "Remember that one Halloween when we told everyone we were watching *Coraline* but we actually watched *Nightmare on Elm Street*? Your moms were so mad!"

I nodded grimly. "I woke them up every hour that night to make them check the boiler room in the basement."

"I lost a whole week of screen time for lying," Sophie marveled. "Worth it, though!"

A vision of Freddie Kruger's fingernails flashed across my eyelids. "Was it?"

Sophie chuckled. We passed The Black Hole without incident. Then I realized my body and my brain were feeling okay, for the first time in days. Regulated. Weird. When was the last time Sophie and I had hung out alone, together, like this? I wondered.

It was . . . really nice, actually. And not awkward at all.

"So . . ." Sophie's voice trailed off as we crossed the next road.

"Things have been . . ." She struggled to find the words. For a moment, all I could hear was the sound of our sneakers slapping against the concrete.

"Strange?" I suggested.

She grinned. "Let's say abnormal."

That made me smile. Sophie and I used to have this game where we'd try to one-up each other with vocabulary words.

"Uncanny," I offered.

"Surreal? Far out?"

"Zany?" I suggested. "Or wacky!"

Soon we were both tripping over each other's words.

"Curious!"

"Odd!"

"Off the wall!"

"Freaky!"

"Spooky!"

We kept going for a minute, until we'd run out of words that matched. My cheeks began hurting from all the smiling. Eventually, I had to ask.

"Speaking of bizzarro land"— I sneaked a glance at her—"is Gus still over us?"

Sophie's face tightened. "If you mean, is Gus still pretending he's never heard of Cre8 or *After Launch*? Yes. Yes, he is."

"Cool. At least I'm in good company. Because he's definitely pretending like I don't exist, either." Whoa. Had I said that out loud?

Sophie stopped walking. "No! Luke. That's not it at all. You know Gus. He's just stressed. You didn't do anything wrong."

I shrugged. If I hadn't done anything wrong, why did his absence feel like a punishment?

But I didn't want to argue. Not with Sophie. "I guess."

"He loves writing our videos. He'll be back."

"Uh . . . speaking of that . . ." I said. "Harper is . . . well, according to her, she's . . ."

"Luke." Sophie pushed my shoulder. "Spit it out."

A vision of Harper, clad all in black, flashed before my eyes. "She says she's quitting acting."

I filled Sophie in on the events of the weekend as quickly as I could.

"I'd heard about the musical casting," she admitted. "Oh man. She was probably so upset."

"Inconsolable," I confirmed.

"Heartbroken."

"Devastated." I loved slipping back into this old pattern.

"So Harper doesn't want to film anymore, and Gus kind of *can't* film anymore because Mom and Dad are being extra nosy about where he's spending his time, so . . ." Sophie's voice trailed off.

"Fifty percent of us are on a break, I guess."

Sophie pursed her lips. "Hmm."

"I think we just have to wait it out," I said.

"Hmm," she said again.

We rounded the final block to school. Up ahead, kids were in a clump waiting for the doors to open. "I'm sure they'll come around eventually," I reassured her.

"Luke."

"It was fun while it lasted," I said.

"Luke!"

Annoyed, I stopped walking. "What?"

"What if we . . ." Sophie hesitated. She glanced at me, her eyes filled with hesitation. But also with a challenge.

I almost knew what she was going to say before the words left her mouth.

"No . . ." I said. I shook my head.

"Luke, let me talk," she said, her words speeding up. "You and I . . . I'm saying we could do it ourselves, and it would still be great!" She flung her arms out and spun around. "Just me and you! Just for one video!"

"I know what you're saying. The answer is still no."

"But—"

"I'm happy you don't want to quit," I told her honestly. "But doing this without them isn't even possible."

"Sure it is!" Sophie was practically vibrating. "We can—"

"I said no!"

My voice was a lot sharper than I meant it to be, and Sophie snapped. "It was just an idea, okay?" she said. "You don't have to be mean about it."

I struggled to take a deep breath. "I'm sorry. I didn't mean to yell."

She was quiet for a moment. Then she asked: "Can you explain why you're so against the thought of me and you doing something by ourselves, just until Gus and Harper get it together?"

To buy some time, I took off my glasses and cleaned them with my shirt, thinking. I mean . . . this idea was a nonstarter. Harper had the vision, the experience, the leadership we needed to actually do this.

Not to mention I was pretty sure she would never forgive me.

I guessed I could start there. Sophie would get it. Right?

I pushed my glasses back up the bridge of my nose. "Harper is . . . I mean, I know she can be . . . but she's also . . . She's . . . I mean . . ."

"Okay, she's your sister. I get that," Sophie said.

I felt a weight lift off my shoulders.

"She's my sister. So I can't. Exactly."

I've always been okay with silence. Not like Harper, who needs to fill every room with sound and energy. Sophie always understood that, back when we were little.

Until.

Now I really wished she would say something, and finally she did.

"It's just that . . . I actually know Harper pretty well, too, right? And I bet she'd be fine with us doing a video without her," Sophie insisted. "Think of it as continuing her legacy!"

"Why are you pushing this?" I didn't get it. "We literally just agreed that we wouldn't do this without Harper and Gus."

Her nose scrunched. "I'm not ready to . . . I mean, it's just an idea."

"No! You're trying to get me to change my mind!"

Sophie stomped and pointed at me. "You know what your problem is, Luke?" she said. "You have always let Harper be in charge of you!"

My jaw dropped. "That's not true!"

"It IS true! You've always let her get the final say."

"No way!" I snapped. "Harper just has strong ideas. She's always been like that. And I've always been like this! You used to understand that."

Sophie's face fell. "You think I don't know you anymore?" She crossed her arms defiantly. "Well, I know a few things. I know you let Harper take charge all the time, even if you have your own opinion. And I know *that's* why we're not friends anymore. Not because I don't want to be. But because you only ever think about what Harper wants."

My brain was shutting down. *Danger!* it bleated.

And for me, there's only one thing to do when my brain goes into overdrive.

I put my headphones back on. I desperately needed to funnel something loud—*any*thing loud—directly into my ears, so the noise could drown out all the thoughts I wasn't ready to process yet.

And then I walked away.

CHAPTER THIRTEEN
Sophie

When the world feels upside down, there's no better place to be than . . . literally upside down.

Up here—dangling from the monkey bars on the school playground, my hair blocking my vision, the blood rushing to my head—the world was as topsy-turvy as my insides felt.

After Luke had ditched me on our walk to school—which by the way how *dare* he—I had walked the rest of the way alone, fuming, wondering how I ended up in an opposite world. Nothing was going the way it was supposed to! Harper, quitting the thing she loved most? Gus, giving up when the task got too hard? Luke, shutting me out? And me, discovering something I wanted to stick with? No one told me this was what would happen when fame came into our lives!

None of it made sense. And I was mad about it all! Mad at Gus and Harper, mad at Luke, mad at myself. Mad that I'd just started to like making these dumb videos, and being famous, and thinking about winning the contest. Mad that all of this was being taken away from me, just when I'd started to want it.

Eventually, I unfolded myself from the bars, let the world turn right side up again, and slinked into school. I slipped into my seat in homeroom just as the final bell rang, and spent the morning stewing.

I pretended not to see any of the Rowan Roadies in between classes, even though they were unmissable: my brother wearing his VALLEYVILLE SOCCER hoodie, Harper all in black, Luke trying to become invisible again.

Still, I managed to cool down a little bit by the time I met Jazzy at our usual table for lunch.

"Did, er, something happen?" she asked cautiously as she unwrapped her almond-butter-and-jelly sandwich. "You seem . . ."

I sighed, ready to spill my guts. Then I remembered I couldn't tell Jazzy the truth without revealing our secret, which made me even more mad!

"I woke up in a bad mood," I finally explained, poking at my pasta. "Don't worry about it."

"Are you sure that's all?" Jazzy pressed me. "I've never seen you this down in the dumps before."

"There's some other stuff going on, too, I guess," I admitted.

"Want me to distract you?" Jazzy offered. "Or do you want me to just be here to listen while you vent?"

Jazzy was the kind of friend I needed. Luke could take lessons from her! Actually, that would be a very cool series of videos for Cre8: *Sophie and Jazzy Teach People How to Be a Good Friend to Others*. Luke would be the first subject.

Maybe *that* would win the Cre8 contest!

Oh . . . I couldn't think about Cre8 right now.

"I don't really feel like venting," I said sadly, putting down my white plastic spork and scanning the cafeteria. I spotted Harper with her drama friends, and Gus doing jumping jacks in the corner with his soccer team. Luke was nowhere to be found.

"Well, then that calls for distracting you!" Jazzy snapped her fingers. "There's so much happening! I'll run through all the latest gossip, okay?"

I had barely nodded before Jazzy started ticking items off on her fingers.

"There's the rumor that Harper Gage-Flashman is quitting drama, but you probably know all about that . . . or we can talk about how Samantha Muldoon and Garth Doherty apparently went on a date! Oh, or we could discuss how those amazing *After Launch* videos have, like, completely stopped, and no one knows why?!"

She slammed her hand on the lunch table, and I—and my tray—jumped. "Oh my gosh, speaking of, you know what I heard? I heard that the makers of *After Launch* are trying to find out who those kids are so they can, like, give them money to keep making videos! Can you imagine?"

I nodded glumly. I could, actually. Too bad I couldn't tell my best friend.

"Oh, I know!" She pulled her phone out of her backpack. "I can show you the latest draft of the video my sister and I made for that *Cre8 and Captiv8* contest! It's not ready yet, but . . ."

She tapped PLAY and I peered at her screen.

I couldn't believe what I was seeing!

Macramé, for those of you who don't know, is where you tie pieces of fabric into special kinds of knots, eventually turning the whole knotted piece into its own item—a wall hanging, jewelry, a tablecloth, and so on. It can be kind of dull to watch, but in the video, Jazzy and her sister, Malia, were so full of rizz that it was impossible to look away!! They were macramé-ing all over the place—as they walked through the park, in between cooking a meal, and even *in* the pool during Malia's swim practice! They had laid a voiceover track on top of it, talking about the history of macramé and how they both learned it from their grandmother, who had been taught by *her* grandmother, and so on.

It was weird and beautiful and inspiring.

"We still have to put some final touches on it," Jazzy explained, dropping her phone back into her bag.

"I've never seen anything like it." I high-fived Jazzy enthusiastically. I was proud of her!

Jazzy's cheeks turned pink. "Thanks. Yeah, we looked at all the macramé videos we could find and really tried to make ours something new. Something unique."

Unique. *New.*

Jazzy and Malia were doing something original. But in our videos, all we'd been doing recently was mimicking what was already popular. Our latest concepts were kind of stale. No wonder they weren't as big.

I dropped my spork and sat up a little straighter.

"Jazzy! That's it!"

She brightened. "What's it?"

I beamed. "Your magnanimous video!"

"Mac-ra-mé," she enunciated.

I grinned wildly at her. "I think you just solved my bad mood. You're the best best friend I could ever ask for!"

★★★

Cre8's mission statement was "to connect the world through creativity and talent."

But our *After Launch* videos were barely creative, and we four weren't using them to showcase any special talents.

We'd just gotten lucky. Our first video, when we didn't think anyone would ever see it, was still the most *real* of them all. And then we'd kind of forgotten why we made it in the first place.

To have fun. To be silly. To do something fresh.

To connect to each other.

Instead, we'd been following trends and trying to shape the algorithm.

And it had ruined us!

But there had to be a way out of the mess we'd made. Messes, actually: our videos, and our friendship. I just knew it. Even if I was the only one who thought so.

I walked home alone after school, thinking. I needed a plan of action. I needed to save our reputation . . . and save the Rowan Roadies.

"Yoo-hoo!"

Behind me, the unmistakable voice of Olivia called out, followed by the sound of two bike wheels screeching to a stop.

I coughed. Olivia's fast braking had kicked up some dirt right into my face!

"Rude," I wheezed, waving my hand in front of my face to clear the dust.

She totally ignored me. "Where are all your friends?"

"Busy," I said, glaring.

She tsk-ed. "Sorry to hear that. Do you need a sitter to walk you home? Or maybe . . ."

I rolled my eyes. "I don't need a sitter at all. Remember?"

"Sure, I remember," she said. "Easiest gig I had ever had, and now it's all over . . ."

Could Olivia be salty because she'd lost a client?

"It *was* a cushy job, wasn't it?" I asked her. "Taking care of great kids like us."

She nodded glumly. "Your parents paid well, and I never had to keep you occupied. It was a dream!"

"You still sit for all the toddlers on the block, though, right?" I asked.

"Yes, but they're exhausting!"

I shrugged. "Well . . . I'm sorry we grew up."

Olivia glared at me. "And *I'm* sorry your friends all ditched you. Do you ever wonder what they're really up to?"

"They're not up to anything," I insisted. What was she trying to imply anyway? That the Rowan Roadies were icing me out? *Betraying* me?! She had a lot of nerve! "They're just . . . busy!"

She smirked. "Sure, Sophie. Anyway, thought you might want one of these. And don't worry, I already left a bunch with your dad."

Olivia held out her hand, and I peered at what looked like a business card in her palm.

> *Lost pets? Missing garbage bins? Damaged mailboxes?*
> *Sneaky kids who are up to no good?*
> **Let the Search Engines help!**
> *We're a team of teens who can solve mysteries and find answers.*
> *Reasonable rates! Fast results!*
> *Local cases only, please, we're too young to drive.*

I snorted. "The Search Engines?"

Olivia narrowed her eyes. "You got a problem with that?"

"Not at all," I said. "Tell Scooby and the gang I said hey."

"Well, your dad seemed really interested in our services," she replied. "Especially the part about sneaky kids in the neighborhood. I wonder why?" And then she hopped back on her bike and took off, her voice trailing behind her. "Toodles!"

I stomped along the street, thinking. *Boiling* was more like it. Olivia made me so mad! First of all, no one had ditched me! And second of all, what did she mean about sneaky kids? Did she really think she could *threaten* me?

Okay, fine. Maybe I had been ditched. A broken clock is still right two times a day, after all.

But I wasn't going to stand for it. Not when what we had was this important.

The old Sophie would've used this moment to run away and forget Cre8 had ever happened. But I was a newer, better version of myself now. I'd learned a lot in the past few weeks, and it was time to confront things instead of ignoring them. Someone had to bring the Rowan Roadies back together. And someone had to win the *Cre8 and Capitv8* contest. Why couldn't it be me?!

I just needed a plan.

Just then, the sun moved out from behind a pile of clouds that had been hanging around the sky all day, low and dreary. Things brightened, and I blinked at the sudden light. Off in the distance, the horn from the afternoon train blared. Distracted, I glanced in its direction, and my eyes landed on . . .

The Black Hole.

The most cursed house in all of Valleyville.

In this light, the sun's rays hitting the modern sharp angles and weird dark colors, the house looked kind of like . . .

A spaceship.

Like the one the Lorgans lived on.

And in a flash, I realized how to solve both my problems at the same time.

CHAPTER FOURTEEN
Gus

"Guess what?" Mom chirped. She and Dad winked at each other. First of all, gross. Second of all, what was going on?

It was finally Friday. I had limped through soccer practice, my bones and brain both tired, then dragged myself home, where I was excited to collapse on the couch and ignore the world for the next twelve hours. I'd already been ignoring Cre8 and the Rowan Roadies, so I was in the groove.

Only my parents had other ideas.

"Can we order pizza for dinner?" Sophie asked.

"Yeah, sure," Mom said impatiently. "But guess what?"

I shrugged. I had no energy to play this game. And Sophie was on her phone, tapping in our pizza order.

Dad jumped in to save Mom. In a singsong voice, he said, "What, honey?"

Mom sighed. "Kids. Listen up. Your dad and I are going to see a movie with Tara and Brynn, then grab a bite to eat. We'll be back around eleven."

Sophie stopped tapping, her head popping up from behind her screen. "Please tell me Olivia's not coming over!"

"That's what I was trying to tell you!" Mom grinned. "You all did just fine without a sitter last time. You remember all the rules, right?"

If only they knew.

"And one more thing," Mom said. "Feel free to invite Luke and Harper over if you like."

In unison, Sophie and I snapped, "No!"

Mom raised a single eyebrow. "Okay . . . I'm sure there's a story there, but you'll have to tell us another time."

★★★

The pizza came and went. I ate mine while lying flat on the couch like any sane kid would do, but Sophie disappeared once our parents left. She was being kind of cagey, but I was so tired, I didn't have enough energy to think about it.

Until my phone buzzed with a text.

[7:16 pm] Sophie: Help! I need you guys! I'm stuck!

"Soph? Where are you?" I called.

But the house was silent, except for that slow drip from the sink in the downstairs powder room, which no plumber had ever been able to fix.

I called her name a few more times, but there was only silence.

And then I made a mistake: I thought of the new writing project Mr. Hassan had assigned us. See, we were learning about how the same story can be told through different genres, and we'd been tasked with creating three potential scenarios for one story. One had to be realistic fiction, one had to be science fiction, and one had to be horror. I'd gone all out in the sci-fi and horror categories, with some really gruesome ideas. Killer robot sharks and ancient spirits and grimy ghosts . . . the works.

Here in my creaky old house, all alone in the dark with a strange text from my sister, while fresh from a writing project where I'd been forced to explore the darkest corners of my mind?

Well, my imagination got the better of me. Anything could have happened to Sophie!

So I looked all over the house for her. I checked the usual hiding places—inside closets, behind the dining room curtains, even under beds.

I stood on the landing of the staircase, split between two floors—I mean, I was pretty sure Mr. Hassan would say this was a metaphor for being split between two worlds—and my voice grew wobbly. "Sophie! This isn't funny!"

I nearly fell down the stairs when my phone buzzed again.

> [7:21 pm] Sophie: Hello? Is this thing on? *taps mic*

Wait a minute. I frowned and peered at my phone. Sophie hadn't just texted me; she'd texted our group chat.

> [7:21 pm] Gus: Sophie, where are you? Did you sneak out of the house or something?

Almost immediately, my phone buzzed in response. And then it didn't stop buzzing for a long time.

> [7:21 pm] Harper: omigod Soph! Epic! We love a girl going after what she wants!
> [7:22 pm] Harper: But wait are you okay for real
> [7:22 pm] Harper: Did you actually run away

> [7:23 pm] Sophie: I didn't run away
> [7:23 pm] Sophie: But I really DO need your help
> [7:23 pm] Sophie: And it's urgent
> [7:24 pm] Sophie: But technically yea I'm safe
> [7:24 pm] Sophie: There's just something you all need to see here
> [7:24 pm] Sophie: Come quick!

> [7:25 pm] Luke: Unsubscribe

★★★

Sophie dropped a pin in her map app and texted us the link. It was nearby, but I couldn't quite tell where. To be honest, I wasn't looking too closely. I was a little freaked out by this turn of events. How had my sister snuck out of the house with me right there? What was she up to? And how did we keep breaking the house rules every time Mom and Dad gave us just a smidge of responsibility?

The sun had set by now. The sky was navy blue, with a couple of white stars peeking through some gray clouds. It wasn't dark out, exactly, but it was close. Just in case, I grabbed one of the flashlights from the junk drawer in the kitchen. Then I zipped up my hoodie and left through the back door, the map on my phone leading the way.

Crunch, crunch, swoosh. My feet stepped on leaves and twigs as I navigated through the backyards of Rowan Road. I cut through the Gage-Flashmans' yard, then ducked under a few low trees, which brought me to the McCallisters' property, kitty-corner to my house. Their house was dark. Under the canopy of trees that bordered their fence, so was their yard.

In the distance, an owl hooted. A car honked. My footsteps pattered on the sidewalks and then sunk into the soft grasses of each yard. I knew that I wasn't *lost* or anything. I was just a street or two away from my house! But creeping through the neighbors' backyards and side alleys and driveways, while the sky kept getting darker, I felt *very* alone. And, okay, a bit on edge.

On my map app, the blue dot grew closer as I jogged across Mooney Street and Hillsdale Avenue, carving a zigzag path through the neighborhood. I was pretty sure Sophie could take care of herself, but I still didn't like the idea of her being out alone. What would I tell my parents if something happened?

I stopped on the sidewalk of Hillsdale Avenue. I didn't know any kids who lived here.

But then the blue dot on the map moved. It was guiding me to walk straight ahead, down the driveway of an unknown house. Then—and this was where things got really odd—it guided me into another backyard, behind a shed that looked like it would fall over at the next strong wind, and directly into the woods behind it.

I peered at my phone, trying to get my bearings. I was in the middle of a small park that was almost like a forest, with just a bit of open space, a tiny pond, and lots of trees. I knew this park existed, but we'd never really come here as kids since it didn't have a playground—just a few falling-apart picnic tables and that dreary pond. It was dark back here, and very quiet, like the whole world was hushed.

The map said I was almost to Sophie. If I just turned left and walked a few seconds —

"Gus!"

Sophie whisper-yelled my name, and I jumped. I moved forward toward her voice, out of the pocket of trees and onto what looked like a wide lawn about the size of a soccer field. (Not that I was thinking about soccer! But it really was about the same size.) I could barely make out the rooftop lines of some houses through the greenery.

And there, in the middle of this green field, was my sister. I only spotted her with the light of my phone.

"What are you doing here?" I demanded. "You snuck out? What's gotten into you?!"

She shrugged. "I had an idea."

"Jeez, Soph, you really scared me."

Sophie almost looked sorry. "I wasn't trying to scare you. Just . . . move you to action, okay?"

"So, what are we doing here?" I gestured wildly around us, as if Sophie didn't realize she'd lured me to some secret park. As I did so, a tiny light in the trees—so small and dim that I almost didn't notice it—caught my eye.

A light that wasn't there before.

A light that was moving.

Toward us.

I flung myself toward Sophie. "Duck!" I mumbled into her head as I wrapped my arms around her in a tackle position. We went down, a jumble of limbs, landing on the cool, soft grass.

"Gus!" Sophie hissed, fighting me off.

But there was nowhere to hide! What wasn't she understanding? Someone was clearly onto us!

The woods, I realized, breathing heavy. We needed to low-crawl over to the perimeter, where we could camouflage ourselves in the brush and—

"Uh . . . hi?"

A bright light shone on our faces.

"Arghh!" I yelled. I flung my hands over my eyes to block my identity. "Go away! We don't have any cereal!"

Sophie rolled away from me—even though I was protecting her!—and quickly hopped to her feet, rubbing her elbow. "Cereal? Gus, what is *wrong* with you?"

"Me?" I curled into a ball on the grass, pulling my hood over my head as tightly as I could. "You're the one who's been lured here by a killer! Go away, man! There's a box of Sweetie Pies at our house that you can have if you just leave us alone!"

Sweetie Pies was the absolute best, most sugary, least nutritious cereal brand you could find. It came in cherry, raspberry, and strawberry flavors, and it was absolutely never on sale, according to my parents. It was also my all-time favorite, but Mom and Dad rarely let us eat it. I thought I was being pretty generous by offering it to the killer in exchange for our lives.

"You have the culinary tastes of a toddler," said the killer. "Also, get up, Gus."

Wait a minute.

A cereal killer who didn't like cereal?

A cereal killer who sounded like . . .

"Luke?" I said incredulously, tugging my hood away from my eyes.

Yep, it was Luke. The light from the old-fashioned camcorder he was randomly carrying reflected off his glasses so it was kind of hard to see his face, but I'd know him anywhere.

"Oh," I said. I stood up and brushed the dirt off my limbs. "Sorry about that."

"Maybe later you can explain the thing about the cereal," Luke said. He glanced down at the camcorder, almost like he was surprised to find it in his hands, and powered it down.

"Hi," Sophie said. Was it just me, or did Sophie suddenly seem . . . nervous?

Luke cleared his throat and glanced at my sister. "Erm. Sophie. Hi. I got your text."

The vibes were definitely off.

But you know what? That wasn't my problem.

"I'm going home." I started walking back the way I'd come. There was some leftover mac and cheese demanding my attention. And of course now I wanted some Sweetie Pies.

"No! Wait!" Sophie leaped onto my shoulders and wrapped her body around my back.

I shook her off impatiently. "You have five seconds to explain," I said.

Luke adjusted his glasses. "Five seconds is not a lot of time. Usually, people offer a minute or two. Just to be fair."

"Noted," I sighed.

"Fine, fine. I want to explain!" Sophie said. "I'm just waiting for—"

"Hello! Anyone there! Sophie?"

Through the woods came Harper's unmistakable voice. That girl really did know how to project from the stage. Even when the "stage" was the forest.

Suddenly, Sophie's plan was starting to make sense.

CHAPTER FIFTEEN
Harper

"I'm here! I'm here! Sow-wee I'm late!"

Up ahead, through the trees, I could see three familiar outlines. I didn't know what kind of scavenger hunt Sophie had set up for us, but it was so fun! And VERY DRAMATIC!

Clearly, I was rubbing off on her. You're welcome, Sophie!

I ducked under some hanging branches and then, since the creepy forest-thing I'd been dashing through had opened up into a grassy area that was too irresistible to ignore, I broke into a run and did a beautiful leap in the air, even though I was wearing a backpack. I twirled. I flung out my arms. I imagined myself onstage, frolicking in a meadow, wow-ing the audience—

Wait a minute. Nope. I landed (not quite as gracefully as I would have wanted) and pushed away the thought.

For a second, I'd forgotten that I was no longer an actress.

The stage was no longer my home.

My name would never be plastered on a marquee, up in lights.

However, in that moment, it was VERY DIFFICULT to remember why I'd committed so vocally to that decision.

"You made it!" Sophie gave me a quick squeeze. I basked in her warm welcome. It was nice to be appreciated!

"Of couwse I made it," I said. "You said you needed help."

Gus frowned at me. "Why are you talking like that?"

I opened my mouth wide and tilted back my head. There, glistening on the roof of my mouth, was a medieval-looking device that would slowly open up my jaw and give my teeth the space they needed to straighten out. My journey into orthodontics had begun.

"You got a palate expander?" Sophie looked closer. "Ouch."

"It's not that bad," I said modestly. (In reality, I'd been in MEGA PAIN since its installation on Monday. All week I'd been subsisting solely on soft, mushy foods . . . don't tell anyone, but I was even getting tired of ice cream. ICE CREAM!)

Gus spoke over both of us. "Sophie, can you tell us why we're here?"

"Yeah," I said, sliding off my backpack and placing it gently on the ground. There was precious cargo in there! "Why'd you run away?"

"I didn't," she said impatiently, which if you ask me, was sort of rude.

Luke said, "You told us it was an emergency."

"I don't think I said that word exactly . . ." Sophie hesitated.

The girl CLEARLY needed saving.

"Well, we're here!" I piped up. "And since it's been a while since we've been together, I'm excited to see you all! Is this an intervention? Are we, like, going camping or something?"

"I'm not sleeping out here." Gus crossed his arms. "No way."

"I don't think we're allowed to camp on somebody's private property . . ." Luke said.

"Can everyone just give me a second to talk?" Sophie said. She tucked her hair behind her ears. Was she nervous all of a sudden? "We're not camping. We're—gosh, Harper, what *is* that noise?"

"Oh!" I hadn't realized the others could hear it. I bent over and unzipped my backpack. Immediately, Poodle's adorable little head popped up.

"Meow," the cat said.

"It's just Poodle," I announced, unnecessarily. I pushed down the zipper some more and found her leash, which I wrapped around my wrist. Poodle climbed out of the bag and began sniffing around, her tail waving in the evening breeze.

Gus looked confused. "You brought Poodle? But why?"

I shrugged. "Why not?"

"As I was saying," Sophie said loudly.

"Is there someplace else we could go for this?" Gus interrupted. He glanced around. The sky was fully dark now, and the moon was mostly hidden behind a cloud.

"No," Sophie said stubbornly. "We need to be here."

"But why?" Luke asked.

"IF YOU ALL WOULD LET ME SPEAK, I COULD TELL YOU!" Sophie burst out.

The rest of us froze. Sophie was SO mad! This was getting awkward!

Luckily, I knew what we needed: a Poodle-omenon. (It's like a phenomenon, but starring Poodle.) I plopped onto the grass in a cross-legged position and hugged Poodle close. I held up a paw and stuck out my lower lip. "Sow-wee, Sophie," I said, pretending my cat was the one talking. "Please tell us ev-ewy-ting."

Sophie giggled, and even Gus and Luke thawed out, both of them joining me on the ground. If anyone ever needed proof that Poodle could contribute to world peace efforts, here it was!

"Okay. Sorry about that. I just really want to explain my idea."

We all nodded. She took a deep breath.

"This all started with the Macarena," she said.

"That old dance Mom and Dad do at weddings?" Gus asked.

I waved Poodle's paw again and used my silly voice. "Meow?"

"You know," Sophie huffed. "That hobby that mostly grandmothers have? Kind of like knitting?" She moved her hands back and forth, mimicking someone weaving two things together.

Gus sighed and dropped his head into his hands, like he couldn't believe his sister.

"I think the word you're looking for is macramé," Luke offered.

"That's what I said." Sophie shrugged. "Anyway, Jazzy was telling me about the Cre8 video she and her sister are submitting to the contest. And it made me think about our first video, and how it was totally accidental. Right?"

We all nodded. Ah, memories! I'd been the one to set up my phone, dress up as a Lorgan, and creep up on my friends to scare them . . . They'd had NO IDEA what was coming for them.

And THAT is what had made that first video go viral: It was totally unscripted. Totally ORGANIC. Real.

I started to get a funny feeling inside. The kind of feeling that makes you wonder if you need to rethink some decisions.

Sophie continued. "It was original. Fresh. And that's why it was so successful. Right?"

"Yeah," Gus said. "But, like, what does this have to do with macramé, or whatever it's called?"

"I'm getting there." Sophie began pacing in front of us as we sat in a half circle. The park was still eerily quiet, and the temperature was dropping quickly. I shivered. I was just in a thin black tee I'd stolen from Mom T's dresser, plus some ratty old black jeans. Related: I was VERY TIRED of wearing all black, but alas, I had a ROLE TO PLAY.

"And our second video was an accident. I tripped and—well, you know the rest," she said quickly.

I burst out laughing at the memory. But my laugh was loud, and it echoed across the grass. Practically all of Valleyville could hear me.

"Shush!" Gus whispered.

"Sow-wee," I mouthed.

"The point is," Sophie stated, "*that* video was also unplanned. And it went even more viral than the first!"

Was she still mad about the bet? I wondered.

Luke just nodded. Gus shifted on the ground. That kid could NEVER sit still! I quickly dug inside my backpack to see if I had anything in there to help him. When my hands came across something small and round, I pulled it out and tossed it to him. Perfect!

It was a tennis ball I sometimes used with Poodle—who likes to think she's a dog—and Gus got to his feet and started dribbling it. IMPRESSIVE, given how small it was! He really did concentrate best when his body was in motion.

Sophie just kept talking. "And then we hit a snag. The two videos we released after that felt a little . . . forced. We started following trends instead of creating our own."

"This all tracks." I nodded. Poodle, who couldn't sit still on my lap, took the opportunity to slink away. (I wasn't worried. She was leashed, and said leash was safe and secure in my hands.)

"Basically, we started trying to game the Cre8 algorithm. We made guesses about what people wanted from us, and we tried to give it to them."

I raised my hand. "I'm still a little confused. And also, my butt is cold."

"Here." Gus shrugged off his hoodie—in between dribbles—and tossed it to me.

Sophie stopped her pacing and pointed at me. "Harper, why did you want to keep making videos?"

Nuzzling into the warm hoodie, I didn't even have to think about the question. I knew the answer right off the top of my head. "Because they were so fun. And *funny*. And because I wanted to be a staw." (I was trying to say "star," but man, my mouth was really hurting.)

"What about you, Luke?"

Luke's lips twitched. It took him a few seconds to answer, and when he did, his voice was quiet, like he was embarrassed by what he was saying. "Because it forced us all to spend time together. And I . . . liked that."

"Gus?"

He took a dribbling break. His forehead was shiny from sweat. I felt VERY selfless for taking his hoodie, because if I hadn't needed it, surely he would be OVERHEATING by now!

"Honestly? Because it was something that wasn't related to soccer."

"See?" Sophie nodded like we'd all said something wise. And HADN'T WE? "We each had our reasons for doing this. But eventually, the reason changed. And so our videos changed, too."

I swallowed thickly. "And WE all changed."

"Exactly!" Sophie pointed at the sky. We all followed her gaze. "Somewhere along the way, we lost our North Star."

"We lost our noth staw," I repeated sadly. To hear it stated so plainly like that . . . well, it really made me THINK about what we Rowan Roadies had created, and how we had let it all slip through our fingers.

Luke cleared his throat. "Uh, I hate to bring it up again, but . . . macramé?"

"You're really leaving us hanging here, Soph," Gus added.

She snapped her fingers. "Right! Macramé! Basically, it's a metaphor. Jazzy and her sister made a video for the contest showing off their macramé skills—it was totally *them*, and it completely blew me away. And it reminded me that the thing that's going to make us win this contest isn't whether or not we've matched a trend, or hacked the algorithm, or whatever." She grinned. "It's about creating something that *we* like. That feels like *us*. That is new and fresh and never been done. And all this fighting . . . I think it's because we kind of got a little lost along the way. Ya know?"

I concentrated on pulling some blades of grass while Sophie's words settled in.

Next to me, Luke nodded thoughtfully. Gus said, "I think you're right."

Sophie cocked her head and put a hand up to her ear. "Sorry, I didn't quite catch that. Could you say it again?"

He rolled his eyes, but he was smiling. "You're right, Sophie."

"So . . ." My voice trailed off. So did Poodle, and I tugged her leash a bit to bring her back to me. "What awe you suggesting?"

Bravely, Sophie faced us, hands on hips. "For the first time, I think I found something I don't want to quit."

Gus whistled. I applauded. Luke smiled.

This was HUGE for Sophie! Talk about a beautiful character arc! I made a mental note to use some of this raw emotion from Sophie the next time a character I played needed—

Oh. Wait.

Never mind.

The emotional journeys of people no longer needed to take up space in my head OR my heart. Because I had quit acting.

For . . . you, know, REASONS. Reasons I had felt very strongly about, at one point in time.

Reasons I was having trouble remembering.

Anyway. Sophie continued: "I get it now," she explained earnestly. After all this time, I finally understand what it means to care about something. To honor the team you're a part of. And I don't want to let it go."

"I don't want to quit, either," Gus muttered. "I never really wanted to." He was staring at the ground, one hand rubbing his head, so that his hair stood on end. And . . . was he BLUSHING?

Maybe it was just the moon moving out from behind a cloud.

A million tiny bubbles began dancing inside my stomach.

I mean . . . I had given it a shot, right? I had MADE AN EFFORT. But drama was in my BLOOD. My BONES. My BLONDE LOCKS.

Luke coughed. "I could continue making videos."

I couldn't help it. I leaped to my feet. "The Wo-wan Woadies awe back, baby!"

Gus cupped his hands around his mouth and whooped. Sophie and I fell into a hug, and then I ruffled Luke's hair until he (lovingly) pushed me away, and then I wasn't sure what to do with Gus, because he and I don't really have that kind of RELATIONSHIP, so I punched him in the arm.

"So . . . we're all back in?" Sophie asked breathlessly.

"In it to win it!" I confirmed. I couldn't wipe the smile off my face if I tried! (Though why would anyone WANT TO?)

I'd tried giving up my acting dreams for five long days. Now, I was SO back!

"I just have one more question," Luke said once we all quieted down. "Why are we here, again?"

"And where IS here?" I wondered. I gestured to the mysterious landscape around us. "Like, litta-wa-lee, where?"

"Oh, right!" Sophie clapped her hands. She beamed. Then she dashed to the nearest set of bushes, where she unearthed a couple of duffel bags, packed tight, and jogged back to us with them.

"So, the other day I ended up meeting some new neighbors who moved to Valleyville a few months ago," she said. "Their names are Selena and Steve. They're old—like, thirty-something. But they seemed nice, asking me all about living here, the restaurants they should try, stuff like that."

My heart beat a little faster. I tugged at Poodle's leash to bring her closer to me and then I scooped her up into my arms. It's scientifically proven that cat snuggles can help calm a nervous mind, and I was VERY NERVOUS! Because as Sophie talked, I began to realize the truth:

Sophie had joined a CULT!

Or at least, she was being recruited into one. The signs were SO obvious! Why else would two old people accost a kid like Sophie? They were trying to SCAM her! "Selena" and "Steve" probably weren't even their real names!

"Anyway, well, it turns out . . . Selena and Steve live in a house that we all kind of know . . . the one that . . . well, I guess it's the one . . . listen, you know how kids make up stupid stories?"

Sophie was getting really worked up as she unloaded whatever was in those duffel bags, huffing and puffing and rushing through her words. Maybe she was the type of kid who couldn't talk and chew gum at the same time, because she wasn't making any sense!

"Uh . . . what are you talking about?" Luke finally asked.

She stopped moving. Slowly, she straightened up. Her face was grim. "I'm just going to say it. But don't freak out."

"Oh, sure, that sounds like the start of something promising," Gus cracked.

"Tell us now, so we can call the police!" I cried.

She shot me a look that was peak cult-victim-in-denial. Girl was in DEEP!

In one breath, Sophie spat out: "Selena and Steve live in The Black Hole and since it totally looks like the Lorgans' spaceship they told me we could film on their property, plus this little park is always dead, especially at night, and there are tons of great places for us to film, and look, I brought our costumes and even wrote a new script and I think this can be our contest submission!"

I gasped.

"Surprise," Sophie added, a hopeful smile lighting up her face.

In our shock, Sophie tossed us each our regular costumes: Lorgan outfit for me, astronaut suits for Luke and Gus. In some sort of silent agreement, we all put them on. (I had to take off Gus's hoodie, but that was fine—my Lorgan unitard was as warm as a wetsuit! Though I have never actually been in a wetsuit, so I am GUESSING.)

But then she plucked out a teeny, tiny silver beanie, one that matched our Lorgan costumes perfectly, and presented it to me. She nodded toward the squishy, soft little bundle of fur in my arms.

I glanced down at Poodle.

Poodle glanced up at me.

Then Sophie strolled over and plopped that ADORABLE silver hat on top of my kitty.

And with a sharp "Meowwwww," Poodle leaped from my arms, ripping the leash from my wrist, and raced off into the night.

CHAPTER SIXTEEN
Luke

The flashlight app on my phone was way too weak for the darkness that had blanketed the park. Er, yard. I still needed to process the fact that we were INSIDE The Black Hole's property line, after hearing so many wild rumors about the place.

But first: Poodle. If I didn't help find my sister's cat, she would never be the same. Poodle was the sister she never had.

Then again, so was Sophie. Kind of.

With our phone lights practically useless in this level of darkness, I remembered something. Four days ago, since I'd had nothing better to do, I'd dug around the junk closet we had in our basement, looking for something to occupy my time. (Also, Mom T offered to pay me to clean it out, and I still wanted that special effects software, so it was a fair deal for all of us.)

I'd found an old camcorder, which was probably considered state of the art back when it was invented in the early 1900s. When I'd shown my moms and asked them if this antique technology might still work, they'd cracked up laughing. They promised me the camcorder was only about a decade old. I wasn't sure I believed them, but after I fiddled with it for a bit, I figured it out.

I was messing with the thing that night when Sophie's mysterious texts came in. In my rush to find her, I took off with it still in my hands. Which was lucky for me, since it had a much stronger light than my phone did, and it had helped me get through the pitch-black woods.

The second Poodle bounced, I thought fast, turning on the camcorder's light. *Boom.* The light was super bright and a nice, warm yellow—not like today's LEDs, which hurt my eyes—and we followed it across the field, to wherever Poodle was.

It was very hard to move quickly in an astronaut costume, in the dark, in an unfamiliar field. I could hear my friends complaining as they tripped over rocks and branches—and in one case a Frisbee—on our way to the tree line. When Sophie was headed straight for a cluster of thorny bushes, she had no choice but to hurdle over them in a back flip.

"Ten out of ten!" I called out to her as we ran. She shot me a thumbs-up. I wondered if that meant we were good after our dumb fight the other day.

"Where are we?" Gus huffed.

"And how big is this place?!" Harper moaned.

"We're technically back on Selena and Steve's property—the park kind of cuts into their yard at a weird angle," Sophie explained, breathless.

I crashed into Gus, who'd been leading the pack, when he stopped suddenly. Sophie then crashed into *me*, and Harper into *her*—it was like something out of a cartoon.

"Poodle?" Harper called. The panic in her voice was loud and clear. I reached out for her hand to comfort her. But when I squeezed her fingers, Sophie reacted with a nervous chuckle.

"Sorry," I muttered, feeling heat crawl up my cheeks. Wrong hand. But neither of us let go right away.

"Why'd we stop?" Harper asked Gus.

I aimed the camcorder in the direction that he was pointing.

Harper breathed a sigh of relief. "Poodle!"

Still wearing her silly silver hat, the cat was walking happily along the bottom of a very deep, very drained, and very dirty in-ground pool.

"I'll just . . ." Harper looked wildly around for a ladder or some way to climb in. But the pool was in bad shape, with cracked and broken pieces of cement sticking up over thick brown puddles, and the only ladder in sight was broken, swinging from one side. Shards of broken glass covered the steps in the shallow end, which were crumbling. The whole thing looked like it had been through an earthquake. Or, even worse, like it was the floor of Harper's bedroom.

"Just jump in, and then we'll pull you back up? Together, we're pretty strong," Gus said, brainstorming.

"In these?" Harper glanced doubtfully at her shoes. To me, they looked like black ballet slippers, but why would someone wear ballet slippers if they weren't a ballerina?

"Meow," said Poodle.

"Do it," Gus urged. "You'll be fine!"

Harper crouched and slid her legs over the side of the pool.

"Kitty, kitty," she murmured. Poodle paused; her ear flicked.

Harper was about to land on the pool's bottom when her hands slipped. Then, with a not-so-graceful crash, she fell the rest of the way, landing on her butt in a puddle of muck.

"Why is this pool so deep?" she moaned. She stood up and tried to brush off her butt, but her Lorgan costume was soaked and filthy.

Gus let out a low whistle. "That can't feel good."

"Get. Me. Out. Of. Here!" Harper began hopping around the pool floor, trying to avoid the other puddles (and who knows what else). In her silver unitard, in the moonlight, she sure looked like an alien creature. In fact, she'd never looked more Lorgan.

"Watch out!" Sophie suddenly cried, pointing to Poodle. After the fall, the cat had wandered to the shallow end. She glanced up as if to assure us she wasn't going anywhere. But cats are sneaky! In a flash, Poodle flew up the side of the shallow end, using her claws to scale the pool wall. Then she disappeared again into the shadows.

"No!" Harper cried.

"Come on!" Gus directed Harper to the corner and, through sheer muscle, helped her escape.

"We have to find my cat!" Harper wailed. She took off, and we all followed.

It was hard to get my bearings, running around in the dark, even with my bright light. We left the abandoned pool and circled back where we came from. Ahead of us, a flash of Poodle's tail disappeared into the trees. We ran!

It was getting very warm inside my astronaut costume. I tried to build a map in my head based on what I'd seen so far, but Poodle seemed to be going in circles. Between the darkness and the heat, I couldn't sort it out.

Once we crossed the lawn, we slowed down and crept into the trees. My camcorder light was still going strong, and it landed on an old, decaying playhouse, the kind meant for little kids, hidden in some brush.

"So random," Gus whispered.

"Selena said the old owners left a lot of things behind." Sophie shrugged. "They haven't been able to clean it all up yet."

"No kidding."

"Shhh," Gus said. He paused, so we all paused, because he seemed to be leading the way. "Do you hear that?"

I listened. Under the sounds of our own breathing and the rustling of our costumes, there was . . . something.

Creak.

Scratch, scratch.

And then: a long, loud yelp.

The kind a cat in trouble might make.

"This way," I decided, pointing right. We moved deeper into the trees. Up ahead, the camcorder light caught on something.

"I see her!" Harper called. She darted forward, pushing some low branches out of her way.

Slap. The branches ricocheted back, slamming right into Gus's forehead.

"Ow!" he yelled.

"Consider it karma!" Harper called over her shoulder.

Gus was offended. "For what?!"

Sophie poked his arm. "You *did* tell her to jump into the pool . . ."

"Hush!" I said. We were closer to the noises. It sounded like something—Poodle?—was walking on a bed of leaves or straw.

"Oh no," I realized. "Harper! Come back!"

But it was too late.

★★★

Gus, Sophie, and I broke through the mini-forest into a clearing on the other side. I brushed some leaves off my head and face so I could see, and then I kind of wished I hadn't.

There was Harper.

At least, I think it was Harper. It was hard to tell at first. She was standing next to what looked like a treehouse, only the treehouse was on the ground instead of in a tree. And she was covered in feathers, brown and white and black and red. I guess because her unitard had been wet from the pool, they all stuck? Anyway, the more she tried to get them off, the more of a mess she made, and now she was almost entirely covered.

And at her feet, dozens of chickens pecked at the ground. *Cluck, cluck, cluck, peep.* They—along with Harper—were penned inside a small bit of yard strung with chicken wire.

"Help!" the feathered creature wailed. "I'm stuck!"

Gus whistled. "What the . . ."

Sophie winced. "Did I forget to mention Selena and Steve have chickens?"

"How did you get in there?" I asked my sister.

"Thwough the doow," Harper moaned.

"Okay, but why?"

"I thought it was a twee house," Harper moaned.

Gus blinked. "On the ground?"

"With chickens in it?" I said incredulously.

When Harper coughed, feathers floated all around her face.

At least the coop and the fenced-in yard connected to it were nice—clean, and big enough for Harper to stand up straight—and it looked like the chickens were well cared for. I didn't think Harper would want to hear those opinions, though, so I kept them to myself. I opened the door and stepped around a bunch of chickens clucking at my feet. All three of us tried to clean the feathers off Harper, but it was pretty hopeless.

There was no sign of any animals except for these chickens. I was afraid to ask, but I had to. "Poodle?"

Harper looked like she was going to cry.

It was time to regroup.

We left the chicken coop and marched toward what we thought was Main Street, away from the pool and the forest. Gus's white astronaut suit glowed in the dark. "We can't keep chasing a cat in the dark," he said.

Sophie stated the obvious. "This is not how I imagined things would go."

My shoulders were cramping up from carrying the camcorder. I was very thankful for twenty-first-century technology. I put it down and stretched my arms.

"Here, I'll take that for a while," Gus offered. I gladly handed it over.

"Hey, what's that?"

Sophie pointed to what looked like a shed. We were definitely closer to The Black Hole—er, Selena and Steve's house—now, because a few lights were visible through the trees. The mysterious property was starting to feel a little smaller, now that we'd covered every inch of it.

"Whatevew it is, someone else has to check the chicken situation," Harper declared.

"Maybe there's a light inside?" Sophie wondered. "We can get you cleaned up, Harp."

When Sophie pulled open the door to the shed, a motion light flicked on. A miracle! We could see!

We crowded inside with relief. The shed contained a lawnmower and a snowblower, but this was also a real workshop, with a workbench and lots of tools. There was a big pegboard in the wall, filled with more types of screwdrivers than I knew existed.

"Okay, we need a plan," Sophie began.

"And a show-ew," Harper muttered.

"Harp, has Poodle ever escaped before?" Gus asked.

She cleared her throat and shook her head sadly. "She's an in-doo cat. She's tew-ified of the out-doos!"

I knew better, though. "Didn't she escape a couple months ago when you left the patio door open?"

Harper waved her hand at me. "Fine, just that one time."

We needed to stick to the facts. "No, she's done it before. Remember last Halloween? We found her downtown near the dessert place?"

"Details, details," Harper said breezily.

"Harper . . ." I said. "Is it possible Poodle actually likes escaping?"

"I won't have you minimizing the pain I'm in wight now, Luke," Harper snapped. She rubbed her cheeks.

There was a bench lining the far wall of the workshop. I slinked over to it and sat down to think.

I happened to catch Sophie's eye as my butt hit the bench. Like in a slow-motion video, her face registered concern, then shock, and then horror.

"Luuuuuuke!" she yelled.

Within a few seconds, I got it.

I leaned my head against the wall of the workshop with a little too much force. So the wall rattled, and a shelf above the bench—which I hadn't even seen—began to wobble.

And a can of paint on that shelf began to teeter.

Who leaves a can of paint without the top on?

I never had a chance, really.

It tipped over, spilling all over the shelf.

And then, because gravity is a thing, the paint poured down on top of my head.

CHAPTER SEVENTEEN
Sophie

If you're going to be covered in paint, the beautiful robin's-egg blue that we were wiping off Luke's chin was a pretty good color to be covered in. At least, in my opinion.

But judging by Luke's expression, maybe he was more of an earth-tones kind of guy?

"It's coming off," I tried to assure him. "Just give us a few minutes."

"I don't like how it feels," he explained. "The sensation of paint drying on skin . . . get it off!"

Harper nodded sympathetically. "I know. You're doing gah-wait."

We found some rags in the workshop and tried to clean the mess as much as possible. Now, the rags were covered in paint, but at least the bench and the shelf and the floor were mostly clear. (Luke's costume, however, was basically destroyed.)

This was a disaster. But what was wrong with me? Was I also having *fun*? I mean, this was definitely funny if you looked at it a certain way.

Without even realizing I said it, I blurted, "Rowan Roadies forever!"

"Cringe," Gus teased.

"Bah-wing it in, people!" Harper cheered, holding her hand out the way a coach does before a big game. One by one, we each layered a hand on top. "On tha-wee?"

"Rowan Roadies!" we all yelled, our hands flying to the sky.

Amidst the cheers, a tiny meow echoed in the shed.

I was afraid to move.

"Did anyone else . . ." Luke whispered.

"Poooooooooodle!" Harper wailed. I couldn't believe my eyes. Right there, creeping up the bench, was the cat who had caused the commotion. Her paws were covered in tacky, drying paint.

Harper scooped her up, planting kisses all over her fur. Other than the paint, Poodle looked basically fine, though maybe a little confused by our costumes.

"I'm nev-ew letting you out of my sight again!" Harper said, snuggling the cat.

Luke sighed. "Can we go home now?"

Luke wasn't the only one who wanted to go. I'd schemed to get the whole crew here, all to bring us back together and use the vast yard—with Selena and Steve's spaceship-house—for the setting of a new video. So that wasn't happening, but it was okay. The Roadies were back, and Cre8 could wait. For now, I just wanted to get out of this grimy costume.

"Let's get out of here," I said. I pushed open the shed door, fairly confident of the direction we needed to go, when a flash of white on the ground caught my eye. "Guys, we can't leave any trash. Can whoever dropped those please pick them up?"

On the ground, spread out in a row like breadcrumbs, were small, white rectangles, leading from the shed toward Selena and Steve's back door.

"Wasn't me," Harper said without even glancing. She only had eyes for Poodle!

"What even *are* they?" Gus wondered. At the same time, he and I bent down to pick one up. Our heads bumped.

"Ow!" I cried.

"Sophie!" he complained.

Luke hummed. "Mmm . . ."

"You're so klutzy, Gus," I grumbled, rubbing the tender spot on my head.

"Oh come on, that was clearly both our faults," Gus pointed out. "But sorry if I hurt you."

Harper couldn't resist chiming in. "You *do* have a hard head, dude."

"Hey, your *R*s are coming back!" I noticed.

She stretched her jaw. "Finally!"

"Guys?" Luke said. His voice was strained.

"I guess your tongue adjusted to the expander," Gus said.

"No, seriously, guys?" Luke was louder now. We all turned to him.

"Sorry, Luke," I said. "Thanks for picking up the random garbage."

"That's the thing." He waved the white rectangle in the air. "It's not garbage. *Or* random."

It was a card. Or cards. Luke quickly gathered them up and passed them to each of us.

Olivia's business cards.

"What the . . ." Gus trailed off.

"The Search Engines?" Harper cried.

I had forgotten all about Olivia's new project!

"It's Olivia," I announced, my voice shaking. "She was passing these out the other day. She's running some kind of mystery-solving club. She practically threatened me!"

"Do you think . . ." Harper said. "Does that mean . . ."

Luke cleared his throat. "It means Olivia was here."

Gus gasped. "Like, just now? While *we* were in *there*?" He pointed to the shed.

Luke nodded grimly. He pointed toward the empty pool, the big lawn, and the forest. "And there, and there, and probably there, too."

"She's FOLLOWING us?!" Harper gasped. "But why?"

"If she's following us . . . she must've seen us in our costumes!" Gus looked stunned.

"I know for a fact Olivia has a Cre8 account," Harper warned. "What if . . . I mean, do we think . . . there's no way she . . ."

"She's going to ruin everything," Gus moaned.

I should have told them when Olivia gave me her card! But none of us were really on speaking terms that day . . .

The possibility of winning the Cre8 contest, of being able to create even better videos with new props and costumes and tools, to keep getting better and better—and okay, more famous—was *so* close, I could practically touch it. But if Olivia found out who we were, if she could *prove* it, there's no way she would keep our secret. We'd be toast!

My head spun. My palms got sweaty. I started to panic. There *had* to be a way out of this.

I took a deep breath, wiped my palms on my Lorgan costume, and turned to Luke with a newfound determination. "A property this big . . . it's gotta have some security measures, right?"

"For sure," Luke said. "I actually spotted an NVR in there, right before the paint covered my eyes."

"A . . . what?"

"Network video recorder. You know . . . a specialized computer that houses surveillance footage from security systems."

"And that'll help us by . . ." My voice trailed off.

"If I can access their system, I can see if Olivia was following us." Luke brushed a flake of dried paint from his forehead.

"And then we'll know exactly what we're dealing with," I confirmed.

"Can we please get out of this open space?" Harper insisted. "We're in DANGER!"

"Come on." Luke turned and opened the shed door again, ushering us all back inside like little ducklings following their very tech-savvy duck mother. "Let's see . . ."

Luke scanned the shelves on the wall next to the door. The shed still reeked strongly of paint, but none of us wanted to open the door for fresh air. What if Olivia was still out there?!

"Aha! Here it is." Luke pushed a couple of containers out of the way. "Decoys. See?"

I peered at the containers. One had a couple of pens, the other was empty. "I don't get what I'm looking at," I said.

Luke explained. "NVRs are goldmines of information. The first thing a good robber wants to do when they break into a house with a security system is find the NVR so they can destroy it—and, along with it, the evidence of their break-in."

Oh, I got it. "So people hide their NVRs so they're hard to find?"

"Exactly. I noticed this when I first sat down over there"—Luke nodded to the bench—"and wondered if it was something important that was just being camouflaged. Turns out . . ."

I punched his shoulder. "Turns out, we couldn't do this without you."

Was it just the dim overhead light in the shed, or did Luke blush?

"Save the googly eyes for later," Harper instructed. "What now, genius brother of mine?"

My cheeks were hot from Harper's ridiculous comment—I'd never once in my life made googly eyes at anyone, let alone at Luke!—but before I could object, Gus cleared his throat.

"Can you access the videos?"

"Well, that's the thing," Luke sighed. Studying the NVR from a distance, he pushed his glasses up the bridge of his nose. He scratched his chin. He put his hands on his hips, then back at his sides. The clock ticked.

"You're killing me," Harper moaned. "I have positively passed away!"

"I'm just thinking." After another few moments, he picked up the NVR and turned it over and upside down, clearly looking for something. "Aha!" He pointed to a series of numbers on the bottom. Then he handed me the NVR, pulled his phone out, and began tapping away.

"It feels like something is happening," Harper loudly whispered to me and Gus.

"Shh," Gus hushed her. "Olivia could be anywhere."

My eyes were still trained on Luke, whose glasses were reflecting the light of his phone and casting blue shadows all around the shed.

"Meow," Poodle said.

"I agree, babe," Harper said in a baby voice.

Luke suddenly shot his arm up in the air, holding his phone in triumph. "I got it!"

We couldn't help it—we erupted in cheers. Until we realized that being loud and happy at a time like this was probably a very dumb idea . . .

"Quiet!" I reminded everyone. Still, I was so proud of Luke! "Tell us what, exactly, you did?"

"I was able to download their security company's app and use this serial number from their NVR to identify their system. Then I just made some guesses about their access code." He pushed up his glasses again and added, "Soph, you should tell your new friends that calling your security system 'newValleyvillehouse' is not the smartest safety decision."

Then, in that second, the shed door creaked open and an adult voice said, "I'll keep that security tip in mind, thanks."

When I'd first rung the doorbell of The Black Hole, my heart had practically beat out of my chest. Since it was rebuilt, every kid in town has heard the stories. Tales of creepy creatures living inside and haunting the block; of mean, old owners who hate happiness; of mysterious accidents for anyone who gets too close. Especially during Halloween season! And still no one knew who owned the place.

But I had worked up the courage to push the doorbell. I had no choice! I just knew it could bring my friends back together (and help keep us famous, too).

To my surprise, a totally normal woman had answered the door. She'd seemed confused by what I was telling her at first—that I thought her house would be the perfect backdrop for a video I needed to film in order to win back my friends—but eventually she made sense of my rambling.

It turned out, the owners were a perfectly nice couple named Selena and Steve. Selena was a vice principal at a school in Manhattan, where she worked long hours. She often crashed at her sister's city apartment during the work week instead of commuting back to Valleyville. Her husband, Steve, owned a travel agency and was often off on adventures, scoping out destinations around the world so he could put together packages for his clients. The house in Valleyville sat empty a lot of the time.

"We have plans to change that, though," Selena had explained. She looked a bit wistful and almost smiled. "We just need to build a community here. It's hard to do that, you know?"

The crazy thing was, I *did* kind of know. Finding your people isn't easy. That's why it was so important to keep them once you did.

Then we discovered that Selena grew up in Queens, just like my mom, so I video chatted my mom right then and there, so she and Selena could set up a coffee date. Then Selena invited me to her back deck to meet Steve, who was grilling. They gave me some lemonade along with permission to bring my friends by for filming.

I might have *heavily* implied that this was for a school project. I mean, I couldn't exactly tell them about Cre8, could I?

I didn't quite mention that I'd need to *trick* my friends in order to get us all here.

And who could have known that we'd end up chasing a cat around in the dark, only to end up being hunted by our old babysitter??

★★★

Anyway, even though we were on their property, seeing Steve and Selena appear out of the dark gave me the biggest jump scare of my life!

At the sound of Steve's voice, Harper leaped a solid six inches off the ground and Gus turned a sickly shade of green, visible even in the dim light inside the shed. Luke's eyes were so big, his glasses couldn't contain them.

"Steve!" I said once my voice returned. "It's me! Sophie!"

"Sophie?" Selena stepped out from behind Steve and waved a flashlight around. "What's going on?"

"Um . . ." How could I possibly begin?

"I take it these are your friends? Hi, I'm Steve, and this is my wife, Selena." Steve waved at everyone like we were meeting at a birthday party or something.

I glanced at the Rowan Roadies. Then I glanced at Selena and Steve. I mean, have *you* ever had to explain why four kids were creeping around someone's backyard, covered in feathers and paint, when it's *not* Halloween?

But this was the type of moment a certain Rowan Roadie was *made* for.

"I'm Harper," Harper announced, recovering quickly from her fright. "And WOW, do we have a tale to tell you!"

A few weeks ago, I would've gladly let Harper take charge. I'd accused Luke of doing this, but I did it, too. Right now, though, it made more sense for me to tell our story, since I was the one responsible for all of this. I *owed* it to Selena and Steve.

It was time for me, Sophie Jane Magee, to find my voice . . . and use it.

"I've got it from here, Harp," I said confidently.

So, skipping over some of the more unusual parts of our night, I explained as best I could how we'd come here to film for our little project, only the cat had gotten loose, which had in turn gotten us all tripped up in countless ridiculous ways.

"And just so I have this right, the cat's name is . . . Poodle?" Selena asked.

"That is one crazy story," Steve chuckled when I was done. "You know, the security app sends me notifications whenever cameras go off and on after a certain time of night. When it wouldn't stop pinging me, we figured a raccoon or something had gotten in here, sniffing around for snacks."

"Our pantry is still filled with boxes." Selena shrugged. "We've been storing some of our stuff out here. Airtight containers only, of course."

She pointed to the workbench. Underneath it sat a family-sized crate of energy drinks, a bunch of unopened cans, boxes of what looked like granola bars, and a big plastic bin filled with cheese popcorn.

"My favorite kind of popcorn," Gus whispered.

Luke nudged me. Oh, right.

"So . . . about that security app . . ." I coughed.

But Steve's eyes were twinkling. "Right, yes. My bad password and all. What can we help you with?"

"Um," I tried. I coughed again. I was about to pop open one of those energy drinks when I realized we'd taken enough from Selena and Steve already.

"What she's trying to say," Luke interjected. Then he remembered some manners. He stuck out his hand. "By the way, I'm Luke, Sophie's neighbor. Nice to meet you. We apologize for all the"— Luke waved his hand around—"stuff."

"Right." I nodded furiously. "Stuff. We apologize for it all. Sorry. Oh, and this is Luke, and that's his sister, Harper. You already know that! I mean, she just told us that. I mean, *I* obviously already knew her name, I've known her forever! What I mean is, she told *you* her name already, so besides her and Luke, there's Gus, my brother, over there—"

"Sophie!"

Luke, Harper, and Gus yelled in unison. The shock of it somehow managed to stop my freight train of words. I took a breath.

But Selena and Steve looked amused. Even *charmed*. Maybe some of Harper had rubbed off on me after all?

"What we're trying to say," Luke said, "is that we'd like to respectfully request access to your footage from tonight."

"But . . . why?" Selena wondered. I nodded again, as though she had asked a wise question. We couldn't exactly say the real reason, with all the details, without giving up our secrets and risking everything!

This time, Harper cleared her throat. She raised her hand, as though she was in class. Loudly and evenly, she said, "It's time I admit that my cat, Poodle, is an ESCAPE ARTIST. The only responsible thing to do for my neighbors, including you, is to identify what TRIGGERS cause her to run away. And I think that, by watching the footage, I might be able to see what set her off earlier tonight, so that I can PREVENT any future tragedies. Thank you for your consideration."

I looked hard at the cement floor of the shed. An ant was crawling past my left shoe. I studied it as intensely as I could. If I didn't, I knew I would absolutely, positively, die from laughter.

With a smile in her voice, Selena said, "That seems reasonable to me. Steve?"

He, too, looked like he was biting back laughter. I dared to peek at Harper. She was still completely in character.

"Let's do it," Steve said. "Follow me. Sophie, can you can leave that where it was."

I glanced down. I was still holding the NVR! "Sorry about that," I mumbled, while Luke helped me hoist it back into place.

It turned out that, despite the acres of property, the shed was just a few seconds' walk away from the back door of The Black Hole. Steve led us into their bright white kitchen, all sleek, with new appliances and gigantic counters.

"To DIE for," Harper cooed, running her hands over the kitchen island.

"Right this way," Steve said, leading us just past the kitchen into a small office.

Luke whistled. "Nice setup."

Steve had two huge monitors on his desk. He tapped his keyboard and they lit up. After a few keystrokes, six squares popped up on the screen, each showing black-and-white footage of different areas in the back, front, and side yards.

"Let me rewind," Steve said, tapping a few more keys. "The cameras move based on the motion detectors, so they should've scanned a few different areas of the property."

We watched the feeds for a few minutes before a movement in the bottom right square caught my eye.

"What was *that*!?"

Steve rewound and zoomed in. We all stepped closer. I held my breath.

On the screen, the video showed what looked like a cavernous hole in the ground. The pool!

We squealed as Poodle appeared, prancing around the ledge before gracefully leaping into the shallow end, deftly avoiding the puddles and debris.

"This is from about half an hour ago," Steve said, pointing at the timestamp in the corner.

"That was after Poodle first took off," Harper said. "Do you have anything from before this? We were in that big grassy area, next to the pool, when it happened."

"Hmm," Steve tapped around. He shook his head. "The first thing the cameras picked up was this pool situation. You must've been too far away for the cameras."

"That's unfortunate," Harper breathed, and she actually sounded sad about it. Almost like she'd been serious about finding Poodle's trigger.

Then I screamed as a gangly, terrifying creature appeared on the screen.

Selena and Steve laughed. "That's got to be one of you," Selena pointed out. "Remind me to get the details of this school project. Maybe it's something I can use with my students!"

"Mmm," I said, hoping she would forget to ask me later.

Sure enough, the terrifying creature was Harper, quickly followed by the rest of us. I bit my lip so I wouldn't crack up as we watched Harper fall into the pool.

"Wow," Luke said, and I sensed a note of appreciation in his voice. "That looks very real."

"You make a pretty good alien," Selena teased.

Harper preened. "Thank you. I practice a lot."

"This footage is hilarious," Steve said.

"It is," Gus said, his eyes bright.

"If we follow this chronologically . . . look!" said Steve. He zoomed in and out of screens and sure enough, we watched what was basically a replay of us chasing Poodle around, from the pool to the forest to the chicken coop to the shed.

I kept my eyes glued to the screen, and I could tell the others were, too, looking for any mysterious fifth figure. But there was nothing.

Until . . .

Right there, outside the shed. The four of us had just run inside and Luke was about to spill the paint. There shouldn't have been any movement at all outside the shed. Even Poodle was inside with us!

So, when the camera zoomed in for a close-up, we all gasped at what appeared.

Just beyond the shed, hovering on the edge of the woods, was . . . someone. Or something. Their clothes were dark and their face was hidden in the shadows. They wobbled in and out of frame a few times before quickly running to the path and placing the bread crumbs of business cards on the ground. Then, like a flash, the figure disappeared.

"Hey, who was that?" Steve said.

"Oh, that was me," Gus smoothly said. We all gaped at him. "Remember, guys? I dropped my phone and had to go pick it up. I guess the camera somehow missed me when I stepped out."

If Gus and I were the touchy-feely type of siblings, I would have bear-hugged him just then. Instead, I shot him a grateful look and nodded. "Totally, I remember," I lied.

"Same," Harper said.

Steve shrugged. "Yeah, this system was set up by the previous owners, so it's a few years old. It probably has some glitches." He spun away from the monitors, clapping his hands once and beaming at us. "Anyway. I know this footage doesn't give you exactly what you wanted, but hey, it was cool to see, right?"

"Oh, it was everything I needed to help Poodle," Harper assured them. Then she swiveled her head and winked at the rest of us.

CHAPTER EIGHTEEN
Gus

I slept in seriously late on Saturday morning. So late that Dad peeked in twice to make sure I was okay.

"You got a fever or something, bud?" He felt my forehead. But I was cool as a cucumber.

Eventually, Sophie knocked on my door. "You up?"

"Now I am," I said.

She took a flying leap onto my bed and handed me a box. "Here."

My eyes widened. "Sweetie Pies? For *moi*?"

"Mom's cleaning out the pantry cabinets and she was giving these a dirty look. I figured I'd save them from her wrath."

I ripped open the bag and scooped big handfuls into my mouth.

"You're disgusting," she said, crinkling her nose when a half-eaten Sweetie Pie flew out of my mouth and landed next to her.

"We share fifty percent of the same genes," I reminded her.

The cereal box empty, I tossed it on the floor and stared at my ceiling. "Speaking of genes . . . I took a screengrab of the mystery figure, and I'm pretty sure they're wearing jeans."

Sophie eyed me with concern. "You know those are two different words, right?"

"Huh?"

She sighed. "Never mind. And?"

Before we left The Black Hole the night before, Luke got Steve to send him all the surveillance footage. Steve was confused about why we'd want it, but when we mentioned Harper's fall into the pool—comedy gold!—he agreed and seemed to buy it. When everyone else was passed out in bed, Luke was still awake, sorting through footage and uploading it all to a shared drive for us to look at later.

We needed proof that Olivia was after the Rowan Roadies.

"I don't have any big insights besides the jeans," I admitted. "But we'll keep looking. This is too important."

Sophie remembered something. "Oh! Luke wants that camcorder back. Do you still have it?"

I did. Somehow, I'd ended up with it when we were all sneaking home.

"I'll bring it over once it's not so early in the morning," I confirmed.

"It's one in the afternoon," Sophie pointed out.

"Exactly."

★★★

After a second breakfast (all the leftover pancakes Dad had made, plus some fruit, a random doughnut I'd found on the counter, and two snack-sized bags of chips), I was feeling much more energetic. Back in my room, I grabbed the camcorder and then checked to see if there were any old recordings on it, just for fun. I'd once read about someone discovering valuable footage on a camera they'd bought at a thrift shop. Maybe there was something like that on this one! It could be an interesting short story to write . . .

Somewhere in the basement was a box of cords that no one knew what to do with. It only took me a couple minutes to find one that fit into the camcorder and hooked up to my laptop. I clicked around and—

I truly couldn't believe my eyes.

It was all here. ALL of it.

Like, every second of our night, starting with Luke walking through the woods when he was first trying to find Sophie. He must have turned on RECORD when he'd thought he was just turning on the camcorder's light.

The video was shaky as heck, sometimes hard to see, and definitely had random extended shots of grass and sky, but still.

I moved the footage into my laptop and dragged it into this factory-installed video editing software I had on my laptop. I was no Luke, but I had respectable skills. I thought I'd just see what happened, maybe make a video to text to the rest of the Rowan Roadies.

But this footage was gold. It was so funny, I started laughing at it—like, really laughing, with tears in my eyes and everything. Even though I'd been there! In the flesh!

It was almost like . . . no, it was exactly like our first two Cre8 videos. Funny, raw, and real.

Which got me thinking. Because I was still remembering what Steve said.

"Hey, Soph?" I called out.

My sister's voice traveled down the hallway. "Yeah?"

"I have an idea . . ."

"Oh no! Does it hurt?"

"Ell-oh-ell. Want to help me with it?"

Silence.

"Soph?"

She burst into my room. She crossed her arms. "I'll help . . . if you finally tell Mom and Dad about you-know-what."

My mouth went dry as a desert. "The writing stuff? I can't. They're not ready yet."

Sophie rolled her eyes. "Come on. You gotta figure that one out on your own, little bro. It's your life."

Then, what was she talking about?

Sophie pointed to my bright green rug. To Messi's soccer-themed aquarium. To my unmade bed, with its black-and-white soccer ball pattern. "I'm begging you. Tell them you need to redecorate your room. This soccer explosion makes me not want to come in here!"

I threw a soccer ball pillow at her. "Then my plan is working!"

Three weeks later . . .

yourmomjokesarefunny: YAY THEY'RE BACK!!!!1111!!! [111,993 Likes]

hannahbobannnn19: Holy moly, this is the funniest thing I've ever seen [415,002 Likes]

User197025: Serious horror movie vibes, I luv it [224,993 Likes]

Ryleeeeeeforreal: they ATE with this video! [109,651 Likes]

AZindahizzle: I'm wheezing this is so real [477,800 Likes]

AfterLaunchFan999: The paint! the feathers! Perfection [95,540 Likes]

123winning456: Slay alllllll day! This one better win the contest! [230,432 Likes]

TheHarbourTriplets: *sniffs* My faves are back, they're really back [345,601 Likes]

OliviatheQueena: Pretty sure I know where they filmed this . . . [109 Likes]

CHAPTER NiNETEEN
Harper

I closed my eyes and breathed in the stale, dusty, kind-of-sweaty smells of backstage. *Ahhh. Refreshing!*

Rehearsals had started a couple weeks ago, and after my brief journey away from the stage, I'd learned how to better appreciate all the joy I felt from being part of this community. Even if it was just as a member of the ensemble.

For now.

I was sitting cross-legged on the grimy floor, leaning against the red velvet curtains that adorned the auditorium stage. They smelled like mothballs, but that was not a problem.

What I'm saying is: It felt good to feel like ME again.

Especially now that I was back to wearing all my favorite clothes. Just the sight of my green-and-purple-striped leggings, paired with my silver cowboy boots and silver sequined shirt, made me smile! I'd buried all those random black clothes in the way back of my already-stuffed-to-bursting closet. Good riddance!

Lila dropped down next to me, ripping open a bag of crackers. "Hey."

"Ssshhh!" Ms. Hopper hissed at us. She was standing nearby, clipboard in hand, as she watched the scene play out onstage. From my perch I could just barely make out Selvi Gill. This was one of the scenes where she had actual dialogue. I crossed my fingers for her, sending a wish to the theater gods that she would do well.

"Sorry," Lila whispered in Ms. Hopper's direction. But her crunching was so loud, Ms. Hopper sighed and shook her head.

I needed to refresh Lila's memory on how to be a responsible citizen of the theater! Just as soon as I helped her finish these crackers.

"I just have to say, I'm really impressed with you lately, Harp," Lila said between crunches. "I know you were expecting a bigger part, but since rehearsals started you've been Ms. Hopper's biggest cheerleader!"

I basked in the compliment. "I had what my mom calls 'a shift in perspective,' I guess."

Lila frowned. "I don't know what that means."

"I think it means I've grown up a little." I tried not to brag.

Shoving the last cracker in her mouth, Lila crumpled up the bag and then cast an apologetic glance at Ms. Hopper, who was now TOTALLY OVER us and our snack break.

"Bummer," Lila remarked.

But I disagreed. I wasn't bummed at all at how much I'd changed. See, I'd realized a few things from my role in the ensemble: First, that everyone involved in a production has a role to play, and they all matter. And second, that being in THIS role for THIS particular musical was a gift, because it left me plenty of room for my OTHER creative venture.

As it turned out, I DEFINITELY wasn't ready to give up on that one yet, either.

★★★

Later, with my backpack full of scripts and books and lip gloss and homework and hair ties and old sandwiches I kept forgetting to toss, I ran straight from rehearsal to the trampoline in the Magees' backyard.

The trampoline was back in action as our meeting spot again. I dropped my backpack on the ground and climbed in, the first one to arrive. I leaned back and took in the view.

Summer was on its way. Soon, the school year would end, and everything would change again. For now, though, Valleyville was showing off its goods, with bursts of wildflowers lining the sidewalks, gardens brimming with bright pink and red rosebushes, and blooming magnolia trees that made me feel like I was walking in fairyland.

Sophie climbed in, the trampoline gently bouncing as she crawled over to sit near me.

"Isn't it just the perfect day?" I asked dreamily.

"It'll be perfect once we have our answer," she grumbled.

Today was the day. Like, THE day. Cre8 was announcing the winners of the contest.

And I wasn't alone in thinking we had a very good shot.

Okay, it had been a WILD few weeks.

Once Gus discovered Luke was accidentally filming the whole time we were on the hunt for Poodle, he went ahead and edited the footage.

And it turned out, it was funny. Like, this-could-be-a-winning-video funny. Even though most of the time our faces were visible, he'd been able to hide our identities through some clever cuts and special effects.

But that wasn't all. The winning Cre8 video needed to be much more innovative than that. Luckily, Gus had the genius idea of COMBINING videos! He overlaid a bunch of the grainy black-and-white security feed between fast-paced clips of Luke's camcorder footage. The four of us patched together a heck of a story. We jointly wrote a script and then laid down a voice-over track, which we each took turns narrating, in addition to using some of the original audio from the big Poodle chase itself.

We called the video "UFO Crash! The True Story of a Lorgan Encounter." And, since it used a cinematic technique called "found footage," where the shots were presented as if they were recordings of real events, it was unlike anything Cre8 had ever seen!

I was really proud of the video. (And not just because, as the Lorgan in question, I was basically the star!)

I was also really proud of the four of us for working together so well on it. No fights; no jostling for credit. Just teamwork and trust. And a LOT of pizza.

Harper submitted it to the Cre8 contest about an hour before the submission window closed. That was a couple weeks ago, and we'd all tried to forget about it. But now?

It was time.

"Hey!" Just then, Luke and Gus arrived. Gus was shoving the remains of a burger in his mouth. The kid had a hollow leg.

"Any news?" Luke asked eagerly.

I shot him a look. "Yeah, Cre8 called me and I just forgot to tell you."

In his usual stoic fashion, Luke nodded. "Just checking."

"They'll tell us today, though, right?" Sophie asked. She was a ball of nervous energy, bouncing around on her butt.

"Supposedly," I said. There was a long list of rules and regulations that we'd had to agree to when we submitted our video. I wasn't really one for DETAILS, though, so I'd barely skimmed them.

We'd learned last week that we'd made the top twenty. Which, not to brag, we'd been pretty sure we'd do when we submitted, but it was THRILLING to get that notification. And so far, "UFO Crash! The True Story of a Lorgan Encounter" had been our most successful video to date, with over six million views. The success of that video had made all of our earlier videos, even the not-so-great ones, go viral again, too. Plus, since our submission, we'd filmed and posted two more!

What I'm trying to say is, the Rowan Roadies were back, in a big way.

We were FAMOUS. Better yet? Our secret was still safe.

Now we had a real chance at the big prize. And the money that would make us become PROFESSIONAL content creators, and help us throw the best block party around!

"Let me take a look," Gus said. He started scrolling through his phone. "Sorry I've been kind of MIA lately. The season ends in a few days."

"Yeah, but then you've got summer season," Sophie reminded him.

Gus shrugged, his eyes still on his phone. "Maybe."

Sophie's jaw dropped. So did mine. We gaped at each other. Was Gus about to quit soccer? This was big. This was HUGE! This was going to set off an avalanche of repercussions on Rowan Road!

But there was no time for that conversation, because suddenly Gus went very still.

"Um . . . guys?"

"Did they announce it?" I screeched. I couldn't help myself; I got to my feet and began jumping up and down, rocking the whole trampoline.

"Omigod, we won?" Sophie screamed.

"Stop. No. I mean, I don't know. That's not what I'm trying to say!" Gus looked very flustered. "Harp, did you read these rules when you submitted the video?"

I scoffed. Rules! "Mostly."

He cocked his head at me. Gus knew my game. *"Harper."*

"I don't know!" I threw my hands up in the air. "I don't remember! We had, like, mere minutes until the contest ended! I wasn't really focused on the rules!"

"I mean, you and I skimmed them, Gus, that day we found out about the contest . . . but remember all those pages of tiny words?" Sophie's voice trailed off, and her eyes darted back and forth between the rest of us.

Luke crawled closer and peered at Gus's phone. "What's wrong?" he asked. I watched as his expression moved from curious to understanding to shocked.

"Oh," he said knowingly.

I didn't like where this was headed.

"What's going on?" I demanded.

"We're in middle school," Gus said.

As if we needed reminding!

"The point, please?" Sophie asked. Her voice was as wobbly as my insides felt.

Gus sighed. "Luke? The news will be better coming from you."

Luke cleared his throat. "It's kind of funny, in a way."

"WHAT is?" I practically screamed.

"Well, we're kids." Luke shrugged.

I blinked.

"And kids aren't eligible to win the contest," Luke said.

A funny, strangled noise escaped from Sophie's mouth.

I straightened my spine. My voice was steel. "Excuse me?"

Gus winced. "I guess we were so excited about the possibility of winning that we all kind of forgot that kids can't really enter stuff like this."

"But . . . the finals . . . the top twenty . . ." My head spun.

"Our engagement got us to the top twenty . . . I bet they weren't even going to confirm our ages until they contacted us," Luke explained. "You know, if we'd won."

"But . . . we're the hottest thing since the Eras Tour!" I said. "Surely they'll make an exception for us?"

"You mean we never even had a chance?" Sophie whispered. Her big eyes were extra shiny.

"All that work for nothing," Gus confirmed.

But I wasn't ready to give up! "There has to be a way," I declared.

"We're just kids," Sophie repeated.

"Our video was never going to win," Luke said. He took off his glasses and wiped his eyes. "Because it was never allowed to."

We were all quiet, PROCESSING that information.

After a while, Gus broke the silence. "Is everyone, like, okay?"

I sort of nodded. Sophie sort of shrugged.

I knew I should be mad, that we'd wasted all this effort. Guilty because I hadn't bothered to read the rules. Ashamed because I'd been so wrong.

But actually?

Wasn't this kind of . . . funny?

"Well, this is perfect," Sophie groaned. "Just perfect!"

I glanced at Luke, and at Gus. At the same time, we all burst into laughter. And Sophie had no choice but to join us.

And you know what? She was right. Here we were, the four of us, under a sunny sky, having a laugh.

This *was* perfect. Just perfect.

BLOCK PARTY RULES

1. No cleats on the bounce house, Gus.
2. PLEASE save some food for the other kids. Limit one hot chocolate per person!
3. Don't bother the deejay. Luke, if you're overstimulated, take a break inside.
4. Maybe put your phones down for a few minutes and be present in the moment? Just a suggestion.
5. Let the little kids get their faces painted first. It's really for them, not you.

BONUS RULE: Just . . . be safe, and be smart. We love you!

CHAPTER TWENTY
Luke

"Aw, man." Gus shook his head in disgust. "But I don't have my cleats on!"

The ticket taker shrugged. "Rules are rules."

Gus huffed, officially too tall for the bounce house. It wasn't easy being a sixth grader.

I knew what would cheer him up: funnel cake. We headed to the long line of people waiting for them.

The day of Rowan Road's infamous block party had finally come. And despite our parents' list of rules, we were still having a pretty good time. Okay—a great time. Even though the music was playing a little too loud.

Valleyville was a town that liked its neighborhood events, and our annual block party had never been better. While we didn't have much money to contribute, thanks to the whole not-winning-the-contest thing, we did want to make things right after last year's disaster. Instead of blowing our nonexistent cash on the biggest bounce house around, we dug through our friends' garages for smaller, used ones, and patched them up with tape and glue. Instead of hiring a celebrity deejay, we made a killer playlist. Some of Gus's teammates and Harper's theater friends had come to help us set up tables and chairs.

And the four of us made a promise to let the little kids cut in front of us in the hot chocolate line whenever they wanted to. So, guess what? The party was just right. Even our parents were impressed. (Take that, Nancy from the big red house up the hill, who never trusted we could pull this off.) There were carnival games, a face-painting station, and lots of food, including the Harris family's famous homemade funnel cakes. My mouth watered. This line was taking forever!

Sophie tapped my shoulder. I raised my eyebrow at the single blue butterfly painted on her cheek.

"What?" she said defensively. "All the little kids were done!"

The line inched forward.

"There you are!" Harper appeared. "Ooh, funnel cake."

"Get in line," Gus joked.

"You're never gonna believe what I just found!" Harper held up her phone. "You know how there's that new social media platform YourMood? Well, they just announced—"

"No!" Sophie, Gus, and I said in unison.

"Fine, fine," Harper grumbled, tucking her phone into her pocket. "It was just an idea."

"Oh, I heard about that!" One of the kids in front of us whirled around to join our conversation. I think his name was Jake, and he was in college, home for the summer.

His friend, a girl I'd never seen before, added, "My dad actually works at YourMood! He says they're gonna be huge."

"Neat," Sophie said politely.

"Are you guys on Cre8?" Guy-who-might-be-Jake asked. "Tell me you've seen those *After Launch* videos? They're the best."

"I'm obsessed," said his friend.

My tongue got stuck. Luckily, Harper was never short for words.

"Totally," she said. "I can't believe they didn't win that contest!"

"I actually heard a rumor that they did!" Maybe-Jake said. My tongue doubled in size again. I simply could not speak.

"My dad said there was some mix-up with their submission form, and technically they kind of won, but weren't allowed to claim the prize?" The girl shrugged, her eyes sparkling. "It's all very mysterious."

"Don't you love a good mystery?" Gus said.

"See ya around." Jake-or-whoever waved. It was his turn to get his funnel cake.

Speaking of mysteries, I still found it hard to believe we got famous without revealing our identities. In fact, we were even more popular now, even though we hadn't won that contest. I finally understood how superheroes felt.

And . . . every superhero battles a villain, right?

It was clear that Olivia was on our tail, but I tried to loosen up as the rest of the Rowan Roadies began stuffing their faces with funnel cake. For now, I could just concentrate on having fun. The threat of Olivia could wait. Right?

Between bites, Sophie said, "We're gonna have to figure out what to say to people who talk about *After Launch*."

"That can be a summer project," Gus said, shaking more powdered sugar on the plate. The funnel cake, brown and gooey, was gone within seconds.

"Speaking of summer, Gus has some news," Sophie said casually.

Gus coughed. He wiped his hands on his shorts. Puffs of sugar formed white clouds. "Um . . . I'm doing a writing intensive in July."

"That's cool," I said. Gus was a joiner. Not like me.

Except for Cre8, I guess.

"He told Mom and Dad that he still liked soccer but wanted time to try out other things, too," Sophie said proudly.

"Whatever," Gus mumbled.

"Good for you, Gus," Harper said. She tossed her hair. "It's brave to change your mind about what you want to do. I did it! Remember when I quit drama?"

"You mean, like, a few weeks ago?" Sophie said.

Harper waved her hand around, dismissing the idea. "Details. I'm just saying, it was hard! Of course, I'm back now."

"Hey, kids!" Mr. Magee jogged by, wearing a baseball cap that said VALLEYVILLE, EST. 1861 and a big smile. "Having fun?"

We all nodded.

"I just wanted to say, great job here. You all did a lot to help us out with planning this thing. And I think it's the best one yet!" He beamed. Mr. Magee lived for the block party.

"You're welcome." Harper grinned.

"James!" Mom B suddenly called. Mr. Magee found her waving at him from up the street. She looked worried. "Emergency! The bounce house is collapsing!"

"Gus!" we all teased.

Gus threw his hands in the air as his dad ran to help out. "I don't even have my cleats!"

We finished our funnel cake, got another one, and finished that one, too. Our playlist had ended, and I could finally hear myself think.

"Well, well, well, look who it is."

I shaded my eyes from the sun and looked up to find Olivia.

Harper waved at a girl standing with Olivia. She had short red hair and a nose ring.

"Who's your friend?" she asked.

Olivia said, "This is Hadley. She just moved into the blue house on the corner."

We all said hi, but Hadley didn't seem interested in meeting us. She kept whispering to Olivia, who looked annoyed.

"Can we help you with something, Olivia?" Harper said with a sugary sweetness in her voice.

"Wow, your voice sounds great, Harper!" Olivia complimented her.

Harper blinked, confused. "My voice? What do you mean?"

"Oh, remember how your expander made it hard to talk?" Olivia said. "I'm just saying, it was noticeable."

Harper's face cleared. "Oh, yeah. All good now!"

"Until your next appointment when they tighten it again," Sophie cracked.

Harper's eyebrows shot up. "They're gonna TIGHTEN it?"

But Olivia forged ahead as though she was the only one in the conversation. "It was very distinctive, the way you were speaking for those few days. Wouldn't you say?" She crossed her arms. The smile was still on her face, but her words were pointed.

With a start, I remembered something.

When we'd recorded the voice-over for "UFO Crash! The True Story of a Lorgan Encounter," Harper had just gotten her expander readjusted, and for a day or so had lost her ability to pronounce her *R*s again. And some of the video had used the audio from that night, where her speech was affected.

Was Olivia about to put two and two together?

Were the Search Engines going to ruin everything?

"I actually don't think Harper sounded that different," I rushed in, acting like nothing was at risk. "Lots of kids get expanders. I think it's something like forty percent. No big deal."

Olivia studied me. Hadley yawned. Harper began peeling her nail polish, while Sophie and Gus looked at me like I'd grown another head. Someone restarted the music.

"Let's go," Hadley whispered in Olivia's ear.

But Olivia stared me down for another minute. I didn't lose my cool. I couldn't; I had my friends to protect. So even though it was uncomfortable, and even though I hadn't maintained eye contact that long with anyone ever, I didn't back down.

Finally, she slinked away with Hadley.

Gus stood up. "Come on," he said. "I think I still have room for ice cream."

I pointed to the cooler in the desserts section of the block, where a few melted ice cream sandwiches were still glistening in the sun. "You want to risk food poisoning for *that*?"

"Nah," he said, rubbing his hands together. "But my mom's got some new goodies in her secret stash!"

We all followed him down the block to the Magees' house, where the freezer was calling our names. The Rowan Roadies. The four stars of the most popular videos on Cre8, even if no one knew it, and the best friends I'd ever had.

Inside, eating more ice cream, Harper swiped through her phone. Suddenly, her eyes gleamed. "You know, if we could go viral on YourMood, too, we'd—"

All at once, we shouted, "No way!"

"It was just an idea," she grumbled.

"We all know what happens when *you* have an idea," Gus teased.

Harper winked. "Yeah, we become famous!"

She had a point. Harper's idea *had* made us famous . . .

And the wild thing was, we were just getting started.

acknowledgments

When Kate Egan reached out to me about a book idea she had—"*Hannah Montana* for the TikTok generation"—I jumped at the chance to work with her again. Writing this book was a balm during a chaotic time. Thank you, Kate, for your vision and support! And a huge thanks to everyone at Pixel+Ink and Holiday House; you've been a dream to work with. Special shout-out to Bex Glendining for the most Instagram-worthy book cover.

Thanks also to my agent, Kathleen Anderson, for all the invisible labor on the back end. You make it look easy.

Speaking of making it look easy, thanks to my husband, Barry Lyga, who will always beat me in a word-count race but rarely makes fun of me for it. Thank you for the advice . . . and all the hours you spent occupying the kids so I could write during weekends.

I am lucky enough to have been raised by parents who took me to libraries and bookstores whenever I asked and encouraged me and my siblings in all our endeavors. Thanks, Mom and Dad. Special shout-out to my siblings (Jillian, Kelly, and Dave) and their fantastic spouses and kids. Love you all.

And finally, thank you to my own kids, M and B, who are the loves of my life.